THE SEED AND THE STAR

JH Tomen

For Katie
You've fought as hard as Eyri
and still come out kinder than the world deserves

et tui amóris in eis ignem accénde
renovábis fáciem terræ

Cover by Karl Nilsson (@sigvardnilsson)
Maps by Matt Dye (@mattdyedraws)
Editing by A.K. Edits (@AdotKEdits)

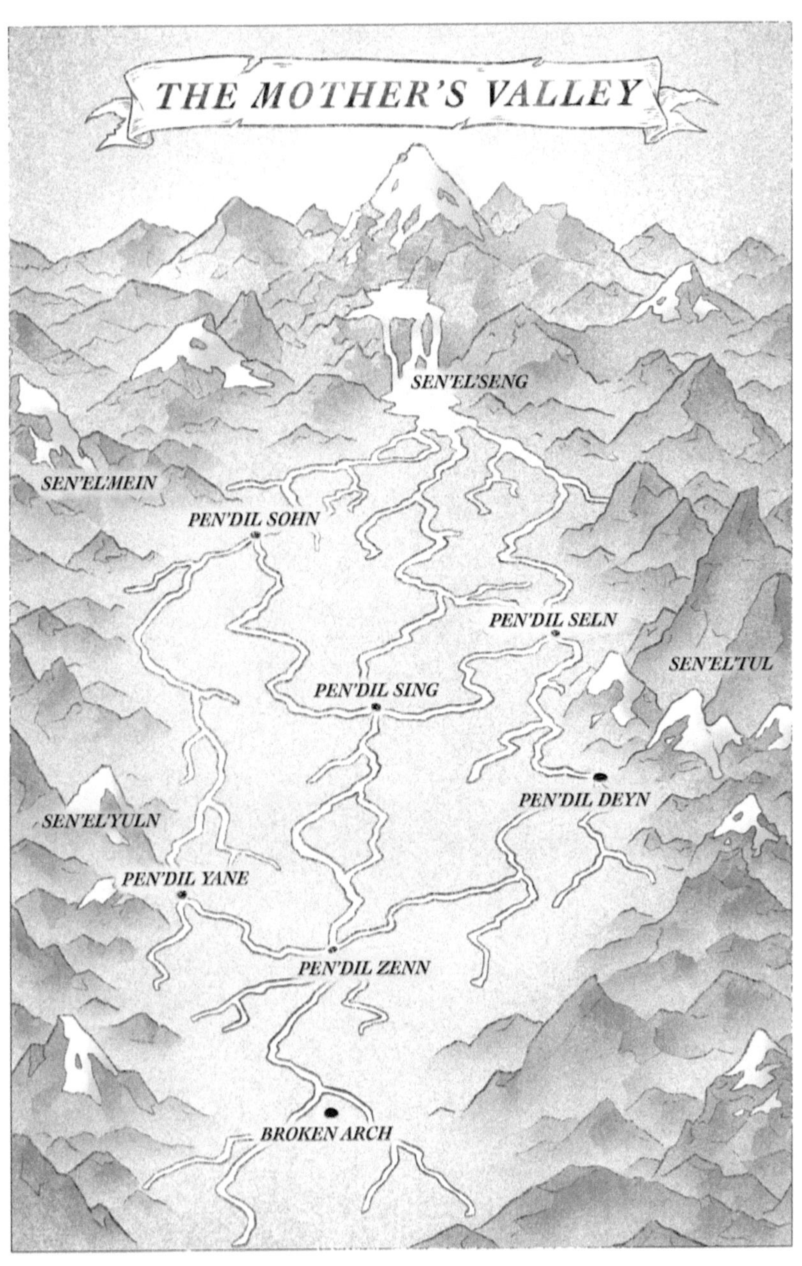

THE MOTHER'S VALLEY
SEN'EL'SENG
SEN'EL'MEIN
PEN'DIL SOHN
PEN'DIL SELN
SEN'EL'TUL
PEN'DIL SING
PEN'DIL DEYN
SEN'EL'YULN
PEN'DIL YANE
PEN'DIL ZENN
BROKEN ARCH

PART ONE

A Journal

The priests told me to leave today. I'm gutted, unable to imagine any life but this one. After leaving Father's artifelary, giving up so much in the mountains to seek the call, it feels as if the gods themselves have rejected me. All for wanting to research the old ways? Aren't priests meant to study the Wise Brothers? Still, they can't take everything from me. I've stolen the journal of Arikai nol D'ek, and I'll uncover the rest of his secrets, no matter what it costs me.

-Journal of Serimh nal Akistore:
950th Year of Finding, 6th of Vindomira (32nd of Perat-kam)

—:—

1

5ᵗʰ of Selomira 979
Rule of the Vindeista
(6ᵗʰ of Perat-kam, 985, 23ʳᵈ Year of Iron)

Pen'dil Deyn - 3 Months Later

Eyri walked through the mist, the ruts of the yak trail barely visible beneath her. Every muscle in her body ached, and even her clothes felt heavy — not to mention the sack of potatoes slung over her shoulder. At least the mist was cold, clearing the fog of work from her mind. She'd been at the docks for twelve hours, almost falling into a trance as she lifted crate after crate. She'd almost thought she was dreaming when the foreman finally tapped her on the shoulder, giving her the potatoes and sending her on her way.

"Money's only for guild members," he'd said, one of the few people she'd worked for who spoke Zennan. "Sorry."

She'd nodded, thanking him in Deynen before she began the long walk home. She'd rather have money, of course, but the guilds were powerful in Deyn, and the only way to make coin as a foreigner was to work for the seedier merchants, a risk she wasn't always keen on taking. But she had food, and she could feed Teros for another day.

As tired as she was, though — the ten mile walk only adding to her exhaustion — she kept looking over her shoulder. Even after a hundred days in these mountains, the closer she got to their hiding place, the more nervous she became. If something happened to her in the city, Teros knew not to come looking for her. But out here, it would only take one farmer who was a little too curious, one yak herder to notice her comings and goings…

She shook her head, forcing herself to keep walking. Teros already thought she was too paranoid. And perhaps she was… But he didn't have to spend each night dreaming of the Masked Ones he'd killed, didn't wake sweating from every nightmare imagining what the Zennans would do to them if they were ever caught.

And yet… Even as the thought of home terrified her, what kind of life was this? Begging for scraps, hiding in the middle of nowhere. Even knowing it would mean certain death, a part of her wished she could go home. Not as a Masked One — she could never wear her own bondage so casually again — but as something, *someone.* If she'd been alone, she probably could have snuck into the kingdom. After all, who really knew her face? But a rich boy like Teros? He'd never be allowed back in Zenn, and she wasn't about to abandon him.

Eventually, the trail began to curve, and she could breathe a sigh of relief, slipping into the refuge of the stone. Even in the wilderness, surrounded by strangers, the mountains, at least, felt safe. This place was becoming a home of sorts — at least for now — and it felt good to be back, to spend another evening by the fire. She came around a huge rock in the middle of the path and began the climb in earnest, grateful even for the ache in her legs if it meant seeing Teros.

Dark stone rose up all around her, unbroken save for a few patches of moss clinging to the rock face. A sharp wind tore through the mountain pass, pulling the mist from her shoulders. She pulled her cheap cloak tight around her, though it did little to block the cold. Would the weather turn soon? It was already Peratkam back home, but in Deyn, surrounded by mountains, there were still snowcaps as far as the eye could see.

The farms were warmer, of course. They were surrounded by giant cobalt spikes crafted by the Deynens, designed to keep the crops growing, though they did nothing to unfreeze the mountains. At least there wasn't any snow where they were staying, but even the foothills of Deyn were steep, though they couldn't hide Sen'el'tul, the giant bald mountain staring down at her from its throne.

"Thank you," she said to the mountain, the words strained by the cold searing her lungs. "For another day alive." *Even if it has no purpose,* she added in her mind. She shook her head. Where had that come from? At least she hadn't said it out loud, hadn't tempted the gods with her sarcasm.

Three months without the mask, three months living with the truth, and it felt like she had no control over her thoughts anymore. Was it losing the Cyran Stone, the powerful old magic of the Elders that had bound her mind back home? And her mind *was* a storm, in ways it had never been before — regret, guilt, and shame all swirling inside her. She was just a human now, a woman with no guild, groveling for bread. She was a criminal. She'd lost her brother and put her kingdom in danger. Still, she had Teros, and she was grateful. Even if her thoughts turned dark when she was alone, she had to hang onto that boy.

As if on cue, she reached the turn in the pass, going north as the land leveled out into a narrow chasm between two peaks. She was home.

Eyri walked along the left wall of the pass until she reached a thick clump of moss hiding in shadow. She put her palms together, blowing between her thumbs in a high whistle.

Kooruuuuuuu. Kooruuuuuuu.

It took a moment — Teros's whistle less practiced — but soon, she heard his answer from the other side. She pulled at the top of the moss, revealing a cleft in the rock where a tunnel ran to the west, barely wide enough for her to walk through. She winced at the pain in her legs as she knelt, pulling the woven moss behind her as she crawled through the darkness.

When she was halfway, light appeared on the other side, Teros standing there with another patch of moss in his hands.

"Welcome home," he said, smiling as he pulled the potatoes the last few feet through the tunnel.

She smiled back, taking the moss from his hands before they hugged. Every day it seemed he grew taller, the top of his head inching toward her chin. They hadn't hugged at first. In fact, she hadn't touched him at all the first month. It had felt…foreign, especially after spending twenty years hardly touching anyone, not even taking Viden's hand until the end. But Teros had woken from a nightmare one night, and it had come as if by instinct, the only way she could think to comfort him. Now, it felt…*human,* like her body was remembering what it meant to have a family.

She looked over the top of his head, holding him close as he whispered to himself, what she called his 'little prayers.' The hugs seemed to help him somehow, to get through the thoughts crowding his brain. She didn't mind. It gave her time to forget the world outside, to find her own version of stillness.

The crevice they were living in was no more than ten feet wide, though it ran back nearly a hundred feet into the mountainside. It was open on the top, letting in the last light of afternoon. There was an indentation in the rock at the back where they slept, though it was too small to call it a cave, at least not like the kind they had back home. Teros had already started a moss fire for the night, and one of his new books was open by his sitting rock.

His whispers stopped, so she patted the back of his head, letting him go as he picked up the potatoes to start on dinner. Had she been so obedient as a child? Even if it scared her to death to think of him wandering the mountains for kindling, she never had to ask him to do his chores. In fact, she had to get him to *stop* doing things. He'd probably even work at the docks if she let him. But how had he become so good, so capable? He would have made—

She stopped, her mouth dry. *Would have made a good Masked One?* It was a horrible, evil thought. That was no life; they were better off free. So why did the mask cling to her? Why did she—

"Are you alright?" Teros asked, looking up from the bag of potatoes.

"Fine," she said, shaking her head. "I just worry about you. Were you careful?"

"Yes," he said, smiling. He was much too timid to roll his eyes at her, but she knew what he thought of her precautions.

"And?"

"And no one saw me," he said, pulling out an especially large potato as he started peeling it. "I only saw the same yak herder that's always in the third pass, but he didn't see me."

"Good," she said, tousling his hair. She passed the fire, crawling into their 'bedroom.' She spread her cloak across the floor before pulling off her plain wool tunic, her shoulders almost crying for joy to be free from the scratchy Deynen cloth. Then, she pulled on her real clothes. Even with all the weight she'd lost working at the docks, the Masked One's robes still fit like a second skin, the silks like butter. She untied her hair, running her hands through it. It was getting longer, past her shoulders, though there was little point in cutting it now that it didn't have to fit under a mask.

By the time she came back to the fire, Teros had four potatoes boiling in their pot, his nose back in his book. She read the title, *Laugda im Lofre,* though she didn't know what the Deynen meant.

"What's that one about again?" she asked, leaning against the wall. She had her own sitting rock, but her back ached, and she couldn't imagine supporting herself for another minute.

"It's a guild history," he said, looking up. "It takes me a while to read, but I don't need the dictionary as much now."

His other books were stacked next to him, ten of them in all. She hadn't read them — hadn't done half the work she should have to learn Deynen — but she felt a strange burst of pride looking at them. She'd broken her back to afford those books, taking some of her most dangerous jobs to earn actual coins. Was this what parents felt like, sending their children to schools they'd never attend themselves? Teros was so bright, he seemed to breathe in the Deynen, taking to new words like she'd taken to swords. Speaking of which…

"You know we have to practice tonight," she said.

"I know," he said, sighing. "But not until we've had dinner."

———

Eyri started Teros with her sword, watching as he swung it over and over. They'd wrapped the hilt and scabbard in cloth from the village to hide its markings — not that it would matter if they were discovered — but even in the fading light, it stood out, the mercury amalgam shining in the center of the blade. The amalgam was what allowed it to absorb magic, an ability that had saved her life any number of times. Of course, she'd last used it killing that merchant Magein during her hunt for Teros, but that felt like a lifetime ago.

Teros did thirty swings in each direction without complaint, though his hands still shook by the end. He was building up muscle, but far more slowly than he should have. She wasn't able to feed him enough, and a few potatoes wouldn't help. She took the sword from him, swallowing her shame as she rubbed his head.

"You're getting stronger," she said, putting the sword back in its scabbard. Then, she picked up the wooden staves, passing him one. They were hardly practice swords — about a third too short and jagged on the ends — but wood was hard to come by in any basin outside Pen'dil Sohn, where they grew the trees. She'd only been able to haggle them off a merchant once they'd already broken.

Somehow, the wood looked even more awkward in his hands, as if he were afraid he'd give her a splinter. He was always nervous around sharp things — holding their kitchen knife like it might burn him — but doubly so when she was involved. She walked him through defensive forms first, the wood letting out a sharp crack as she struck at him again and again. She only got him on the arm once. Unfortunately, even when blocking, he cowered too much.

"You have to have strength in your core when you block," she said, poking him in the stomach as she firmed up his shoulders. "If you're not ready to spring back and swing yourself, you're just buying time."

He did as she said, shifting his stance.

"Buying time isn't so bad, though, right?" he asked. "I only have to fight long enough for you to come."

"I won't always be here," she said with a sigh. "Besides, sword fights are just as much luck as skill, and I won't have anyone getting lucky with you."

She twisted quickly, poking him in the kidney with her stick.

"Fine," he said, rubbing his side. "But I don't think I'll ever be good at this."

"You *will*."

She thought of Viden suddenly, the old man never far from her mind these days. She remembered something he'd told her in the war, something she'd remembered even as a girl.

"There will come a time when the world tries to break you, Teros, when you'll wish you were stronger. I know you want to change things, but changing things takes strength. So, I'll give you some advice a friend of mine once gave me. Take everything you wish you had, everything you wish you were, and turn it into fire. Burn so bright they can't ever put you out."

He met her eyes, a spark of defiance in them, but he nodded. Sometimes, late at night, he talked to her about Zenn, how he wished things could be different. He thought there was another way, a way without swords, without Masked Ones in bondage to the crown. If only she believed him. If only Zenn didn't bring him so much pain she couldn't fix.

"Alright," she said, looking at the crack of sun still left over the chasm. "Back to your books. That's enough for today."

Teros finally smiled, scampering to his book and his rock. She smiled herself, shaking her head as she hid her sword again. It wasn't like he had no form, he just wasn't ready to defend himself. Apparently, his uncle had tried to teach him the basics, too — not that it made her feel much better… Elin nir Dek'rc, the Duke of Remembrance, was an evil man, and one any smart Masked One learned to avoid. Each of the six dukes were dark in their own way, but everything surrounding Teros's capture back in Zenn had only raised more questions. Dek'rc had been connected to the serosine, hadn't he? The metal was supposed to be outlawed after the war, and she'd seen too many Masked Ones die as the serosine blocked their magic. And the things Small Jerin had said at Maegin's warehouse, the connection to 151…

No, she thought. That wasn't her job anymore. Even if she longed to atone for what she'd done to her kingdom — even if she'd do it all over again to save

Teros — she was here now. There *was* a rot in Zenn, one she wished she could have dug out. Maybe then her suffering would have served a purpose, maybe she'd be more than some useless woman hiding in the mountains. But what mattered now was Teros. Even if she was nothing, Teros wasn't, and as much as it shamed her to be teaching him the same things as his uncle, he needed to know how to fight.

Still, as he sat on his rock, a little boy eagerly trying to avoid bed, she wished it wasn't so. He shouldn't have to fight, shouldn't have to know the pain and darkness of the world. Could she ever hope to take his place? To be the fire pushing back the shadows on his life? She would do anything to keep him how he was, a tiny spark in a mountain cave.

2

Elin nir Dek'rc, the Duke of Remembrance, sat in his study in the city staring into his desk. Carved from a solid tree trunk from Sohn, it was a luxury few men could even imagine, let alone afford. Still, gazing into its glossy surface, he paid it no mind. There was much to think about — almost too much for any mortal man to juggle — so he turned inward, to his power, to the essence of the gods.

With his right hand, he unconsciously stacked a half-dozen flat stones, gluing them together with Permanence. Once they were joined, he released them, letting them skitter onto the surface of the desk as he began the process again. He could feel the Passing in his muscles rooting him to his chair, but slowing his body seemed to free his mind, allowing him to think through everything again.

He had hidden so much serosine in the basin, it was getting hard to keep track. Especially after he'd let that *keroshai,* 732, kill Maegin. Still, the man had served his purpose, and he probably had enough of the metal for two armies. The question now was how to get it to Sing — especially without his rivals noticing. They were all on edge, especially after that…*unusual* voting. In some ways, it had been almost inspiring, seeing the Iron King with fire behind his eyes again. He'd sat the dukes down like schoolchildren in the throne room, berating them for letting things get so out of control.

In the end, of course, they'd had no choice but to vote for Surah nir Cosk for the fourth time, the tantalizing vessel of Teros masquerading as Bital, the king's lost son, slipping from the old man's grasp. Of course, Elin had lost his own chance at controlling the throne then, but it didn't sting as badly as it had in 969, after he'd miscalculated so badly during the war. But he'd been a young man then, and his skill hadn't yet caught up to his ambition.

Besides, it wasn't as if the boy had done him no favors. Destroying the temple and taking a dozen Masked Ones with him? He couldn't have planned it better himself! And now, the king was rotating the Masked Ones to the ponds, terrified they'd stage an uprising — or worse. But the king had only ever had eyes for his little toy wagons, and he knew nothing of magic. Without the Cyran Stone, the Masked Ones were in disarray, and he had just the kind of firm hand they'd need to guide them. Especially with Keroes nir Sen'l dead, and a puppet on the blue throne in his place. He—

There was a knock on the door. Elin quickly released the tower of stones, scattering them across his desk. He also took the last potato wedge from his desk, popping it in his mouth as he swallowed without chewing. Those closest to him cared little for the clean lines of the old ways — magicians and demons with no room in between — but this was no time to grow careless either. At least it was potato, cursed food. Unpopular with the others in the royal houses, he'd learned the hard way not to burn food he'd have to stuff down his throat at a dinner party...

"Enter," he said in a clear voice, channeling Flow as he finally stood from his desk, the stiffness leaving his limbs.

151 entered, standing at attention. Always a beady-eyed grifter, his pet Masked One was even more so now. He liked getting his table scraps from the powerful well enough, but the incident at the temple had proven the man had no stomach for bloodshed. Still, it was no matter. He had plenty of dogs in his kennel — even if he didn't have time to train them all.

"The High Priest is here," 151 said, bowing.

"Very well," Elin said, heading into the hallway as he gestured for 151 to follow.

"He doesn't trust me yet," 151 whispered, catching up. "And it seems he knows about Keroes nir Sen'l's serosine blade. They all do — though they don't know it came from you yet. It seems to be cowing the more...rebellious in the tower, but it's only a matter of time until a royal inquest is—"

"I have it handled," he said sternly, meeting 151's eyes. "Don't lose your nerve now. Do you still want to be at the top when my work is done?"

"Yes," the Masked One said immediately.

So, his greed was still stronger than his fear. *Good.* He would make sure 151 didn't survive that long, but it was good to keep him hungry while he was useful.

They came to the grand stairwell, the new High Priest, Tris'ka nir Irmun, standing below. The man looked up when he heard their footsteps, his face in rapture. The front hall was a good place to meet men like Tris'ka. The walls were lined with all his artifels, pumping water and heat throughout the house as he burned an impossible wealth of food on their dials. Everyone obsessed over the king and the priests, but the dukes were the true backbone of Pen'dil Zenn.

"Your Grace!" he called down, putting a smile on his face. "You bless us with your presence."

He reached the bottom of the stairs, dropping into a quarter bow as 151 actually *knelt,* as if he were in the throne room. The effect, of course, was predictable, the High Priest glowing. Somehow, this man was even more pious than Keroes nir Sen'l — something he hadn't thought possible — and showing even the bare minimum of decorum lulled him into a stupor.

"Please, sit," Elin said, gesturing toward the chairs he'd had set up in the middle of the room.

Tris'ka sat, uncomfortably shifting his stole, his neck clearly not yet used to the weight. Perhaps it itched his skin too, a reminder that his stole was new, hastily sewn after Keroes nir Sen'l's was burned to ash at the temple.

"Thank you for seeing me," the High Priest said. "I understand you're a busy man."

"Never too busy for what really matters."

The priest smiled, blinking. He'd clearly gotten too used to begging for scraps at higher tables. He wasn't used to being able to warrant a meeting, let alone the avalanche of flattery about to come his way. Elin rang a bell, his servants hurrying through the door with tea. Another point for piety. Never serve a priest food between meals. He didn't even use 151 as a servant — though that was particularly effective at cowing lesser nobles.

"I'm here about the Royal Inquest," Tris'ka said, taking a sip of his tea. He looked into his cup for a moment, bewildered. Clearly, he hadn't expected to be served his favorite tea either. He had much to learn, but at least there were willing teachers at hand. "It's like a snake with two heads, everyone seeming to serve a different master. I wanted to see if you had any...*privileged* information you could share."

"I'm glad you've come," Elin said, nodding as he put a hand to his heart. "I've been eager to solidify our friendship. Of course, I would share anything I knew with a holy man such as yourself. Unfortunately, I've found things as muddied as you have. We're wandering the dark like newborn cave fish."

He took his own sip of tea, though the dandelion petals tasted foul. If only he hadn't traveled so widely in his youth...

"However, I will be heading to Pen'dil Sing soon. The king has been pleased with my ambassadorship to Deyn all these years, and he wants me to assess the truth of the situation in the north. I'll send for you as soon as I know more."

"But..." he added, leaning forward as if he had a secret, the priest mimicking him. "If I can share my personal thoughts? I don't think Sing did this. I've read every report from that horrible day at the temple, and they say the man — if he *was* a man — had no accent. I know you've always been more...devout than your predecessor, thank the Elders, but I'm afraid we must have sparked the wrath of the Sacred Mother. All these years with the Iron King, defying nature..."

He let that hang in the air.

"Yes," the High Priest said, nodding slowly. Keroes nir Sen'l had kept Tris'ka in a corner of the Little Tower his whole career, but even he wouldn't be naive enough to have missed the bad blood between his predecessor and the king. "I think you're right. Thank the gods there are good men like you still in the kingdom."

Elin rang the bell again, his servants coming in with a wrapped package. You couldn't feed a priest between meals, but no one ever said you couldn't bribe them with something for later.

"I'm afraid I must start packing," Elin said, standing, "but since the gods saw fit to bring you to me between meals, I thought it only right to send you back to the tower with something for later."

"You honor me," the High Priest said, taking the package reverently.

Elin bowed, keeping one hand over his heart as 151 escorted the High Priest out. Tris'ka nir Irmun would prove useful, alright, even if he was just moss to be burned. Still, he liked to think he knew the best use of a man when the time came. After all, not just anyone could do this work, deciding who was expendable as they saved the world. Even Teros, poor boy, hadn't been worth sparing, and he'd actually been fond of the lad. But he was Elin nir Dek'rc, his heart made from the steel of mountains. He'd save the Mother's Valley, and he could pick up the pieces when he was done.

3

7ᵗʰ of Selomira 979
Rule of the Vindeista
(8ᵗʰ of Perat-kam, 985, 23ʳᵈ Year of Iron)

Serimh stood in the orange glare of the forge, tapping his foot as he tried to keep the fools from ruining the serosine. The moment he'd perfected these new parameters, the zinc knights had forced him into production, creating an ungodly amount of the stuff at breakneck speed. But that meant precision, something the hardheaded *fa'ncoli* in the military knew nothing about.

Still, he'd studied the Elders long enough to know the petty failings of mortals could never dull the glory of the forge. Set into the black stone of the waterfalls, it was the size of a cottage and shaped like a vase. Made entirely of metal, its sacred swirl of zinc and cobalt from the city's pillars was impossible to melt, no matter how hot the furnace glowed. It was covered in runes and dials, and even as its bellows roared with heat from steam vents under the mountain, the metal never changed from its glimmering silver.

"Ve'ricka!" Serimh called, waving a hand at the forewoman.

The woman scowled, wiping a hand across her brow as she stalked over from beside the forge where she was helping adjust the bellows with a long crank. She had been ordered to obey Serimh by her precious zinc lordlings, but it didn't mean she would be happy about it. Not to mention how hard they were being worked the day before the holiday…

"What now?" she asked. "We're following your instructions, aren't we?"

"Not quite," Serimh said, pointing to the clock set into the rock. At least *that* was something accurate in this bloody place. He had grown up in his father's artifelary, and he knew there was no greater clock in Deyn, the gears kept perfectly wound by the forge's steam. "It's exactly ten minutes at the first temperature, and then five and a half at the second."

"Which is what we bloody did," she said, gesturing at the clock. But the second hand was still only three quarters of the way to the tenth minute.

"You have fifteen seconds, so why did you start adjusting the bellows?"

"It takes—" she started to say, but he put up a hand.

"Must I remind you how important this project is to the Zinc Lords? If anyone could make serosine, you'd see it on every corner. We'll finish this batch as is, but if the quality is low, I'll be telling your bosses why."

Her jaw bulged as she bit her tongue, but the woman still nodded. Young as she was, there was no one in Deyn who didn't understand the importance of serosine, its powers — and failures — deciding the war against the Zennans all those years ago.

"Very well," she forced out as she walked away.

Precision. It was the language of the gods. If men wanted to be more than beasts, they needed to be perfect, to emulate something they were not. It had been nearly thirty years since he'd discovered serosine in the journal of Arikai nol D'ek — thirty years since they'd torn him from the priesthood — and still, he hardly understood it. The fact that regular cobalt would somehow transform in the sacred forge, but only at specific temperatures and phases... It was beyond his comprehension. Yet yearning for the gods seemed to be the only thing Deyn had left — the only thing *he* had left.

Over the next five minutes, his eyes never left the forge, as if his stare might somehow hold back the workers' sheer incompetence. Still, as the smiths prepared to finish the batch, he started to feel...*excited.* He'd been a prisoner to the zinc army for all these years, but for the first time in ages, he felt hope.

He'd believed in their work in the beginning, of course. It was after the Great Freeze, when all of Deyn had mobilized to prevent another famine. After all, his own discoveries had led them to the cobalt spikes, allowing his people to never fear winter again. It was only after his second discovery, the serosine, when things grew darker. The building of the dam, the war with Zenn — and so many years a prisoner, to himself as much as to the Zinc Lords.

As he grew older, he began to realize he'd overstayed his welcome, had waited too long for the gods to come to him. Even after the war, when everything was chaos — and escape would have been easy — he'd stayed. Back then, of course, he'd justified it, looking to rebuild. And his research, his precious research! After all, it was his love of science — and his desire to know the gods — that had given his kingdom even the meager power it still had.

But now... Now, all he wanted to do was flee. War was coming, and he needed to be gone before it came. Unfortunately, his needs multiplied faster than the years: staff, equipment, a research budget. Still, there were other basins, other pillars he could use to seek the gods. He just needed one more win. This time, if he did the impossible and he made the knights their serosine again, perhaps his skill would finally buy his freedom.

The smiths began to crank the wheel, tipping the forge's internal basin forward. Molten metal poured from the forge's lip, filling molds before the workers dunked them into the water basin below. The metal hissed as it reached the inky water, the purified cesium giving the metal its most important burst of magic as it cooled into the molds.

He finally moved, having to keep himself from kneeling down as the smiths cranked the mold up out of the water. They were only making simple blocks at this stage, but — mistakes aside — he could already tell the serosine was *marvelous*. The silvery metal shimmered in the glow of the forge, seeming to bend the light. Perhaps it was foolish to love something that had caused so much death, but it seemed he'd never lose his passion for his creations.

He pulled on his gloves, picking up the block. It was no larger than his chest — the small batches another cost of its precision — but it was strangely light, much lighter than the initial cobalt had been.

"Well?" Ve'ricka asked, breaking through his reverie.

"Decent," he said, handing it to her. "Just get the times right on the next batch."

And it *was* decent, at least to his most recent specifications. Who knew how the Zinc Lords would use it — and keep the masked demons from melting it down as easily as they had during the war. He'd made it stronger, but was anything strong enough for what was coming? Fortunately, that wasn't his problem.

He turned to go back to his station when he noticed a knight by the door. Unlike the usual forge guards, this one wore full plate, the zinc king's pin on his cloak. Serimh had to swallow a lump in his throat, even as his jaw clenched in anger.

"Two decades of imprisonment isn't enough to earn some trust?" Serimh said sharply as he walked up — though he stopped out of range of the man's curving zinc sword. "I'll have you know the forge workers are bumbling enough without prying eyes."

The knight chuckled, moving his eyes over Serimh, the rest of his body like a statue — a dangerous, coiled snake of a statue.

"I hardly think being one of the richest men in the city amounts to imprisonment."

Serimh's mouth fell open. How would a mere knight know about that? Not that their cursed blood money could even be used! It was locked on a guild ledger — which was apparently monitored even more closely than he thought. He'd only recently tried to access a large sum of it for his research and been promptly denied. They'd always paid his basic expenses easily enough, but the guild stewards had made clear what they thought of him trying to take out more than normal. And now they were airing his business to their dogs?!

Perhaps he'd always be too naive for this life. There was something money did to a man to blind him. But now, at least, he could finally see. He'd never truly be free, never truly be able to access the riches they'd promised him. He'd certainly never be able to leave the city with his money on their bloody ledger, and he'd never get back to the life of pure research he'd craved so badly in the priesthood. They were watching him too closely with the serosine, but when it was done, he'd have his chance, wouldn't he? After all, if serosine meant war, and war meant chaos…

"Well, see how you like your vocation being taken away," Serimh spat. "Now, what do you *want?*"

The knight unfolded his hands, apparently done toying with his prey.

"Don't be surprised, priest. The lords want to know how production is going."

"Well, obviously," Serimh said, gesturing to the small but growing pile of serosine blocks. "We'll be done in a matter of days. But you should warn your masters for me. This is higher quality than the metal we made during the war. If they try to make swords with it, they'll need to tell me."

"I'll pass along the message."

With that, the knight left, disappearing back into the shadows.

Serimh went back to his spot, prepared to bark an order, but Ve'ricka was watching him with a smile.

"Looks like we all answer to someone!" she yelled over the roar of the forge.

He certainly did, and it seemed he always would.

4

Eyri led Teros through the mountains, her head on a swivel in the darkness. Meanwhile, he hummed behind her, overjoyed to be leaving the cave. How had she let herself be talked into this? He'd been working on her since the morning, trying to convince her to celebrate the Deynen holiday. Perhaps she would have been able to say no to any other child, but Teros was so obedient, it made it nearly impossible to ignore a direct request. Not that he'd been *particularly* direct... Still, how could she live with herself if she let him down?

She'd come out of their little bedroom in the rocks, finding him already at the fire, boiling a potato for her. He'd been whispering to himself, his book in hand, though he stopped as he noticed her.

"Interesting," he'd said quietly. "I guess the Deynens have one of their big holidays today. The Day of Joy... I've never heard of it before."

He'd turned the book toward her, as if she could make out the Deynen script. Of course, she was overjoyed to see him talking, so she'd sat down next to him, leaning over the page.

"Really? Tell me about it."

He'd gone on at length about the Snow Father and his founding of the city. Of course, in Zenn, they believed only their Elders had followed the true will of the gods, finding the most sacred of the basins. But what was a little heresy after everything she'd done? He'd started talking about the Deynen celebrations, with their giant bonfires, fireworks, and oatcakes. And by the time she left to look for work, he'd been staring up at the crack of sky so sadly, she'd known she couldn't skip the holiday entirely.

Unfortunately, there'd been barely any work to be had, the city more or less shutting down for the day. There was some kind of parade in the city center, but she'd hardly been able to reach the First Ward for the crowds. Thankfully, she'd finally found some soldiers sweeping up after the crowds, and they'd actually given her a coin to do their job for a few hours. It was a strange way to use soldiers, though knowing the Deynens, it could have been some kind of metaphor, a reminder to serve the people. Finally, the sun nearly setting, she'd used her coin on one of the strange little oatcakes, marching back to find Teros.

Now, she just had to hope she could find somewhere safe to watch the fireworks. She'd seen the people in Hv'rano, the nearby village, setting some up. To her, of course, they'd seemed ominous, like siege equipment, the Deynens preparing to blast the sky with fire. She just hoped they didn't have to actually leave the mountains to watch them. She wouldn't risk actually taking Teros near the town — after all, if they could see the townsfolk, it meant they could be seen too. Even if their view was blocked somewhat by the mountains, though, it was better than nothing.

Finally, rounding one of the smaller mountains, the path they were on ran downward, the lights of the village suddenly visible. She motioned for Teros to stop, sinking to the stone so she could scout it out. She could see the shapes of people moving between the buildings. There were dozens and dozens of them, gathering around a giant bonfire in the central square. Shielding her eyes from the light, she looked around the hills. There were some homes in the distance, to the south of the village, but they were dark, everyone clearly down at the celebration. And otherwise, the cliff faces were empty, no figures moving on the trails that laced the mountainside.

"Alright," she whispered, crawling back to Teros. "We can watch from here if we stay out of sight. I'm sure they'll start soon."

She leaned against a nearby boulder, patting the ground next to her. Their backs to the village, they had a view of the night sky, the infinite darkness ablaze with thousands of stars. Teros sat, scooting across the stone until he leaned against her. She put her arm around him, suddenly ashamed at making this brilliant boy sit in the chilly night. He pulled the oatcake from his pocket, having claimed he wanted to save it for "the festival."

"Here," he said, tearing it in half and offering part to her.

"No, thanks, I lost oat to the Passing," she lied. She'd lost plenty of foods, but oddly oat wasn't one of them. Of course, they grew a lot more oats in Deyn than Zenn, so maybe it was simply luck. Or perhaps it was climate, the warmer weather back home more suited to fruit. After all, it wasn't like she'd ever be able to eat grapes again. Perhaps with the zinc knights and the cold weather, the Deynens really only needed Identity — though everyone knew their food lacked power, the magic supposedly coming from the swords themselves.

"Oh, I'm sorry," Teros said, looking down at the sad little cake. He moved to put it away, but she grabbed his hand.

"Don't be, I knew I couldn't eat it when I bought it, silly. It's still fun to watch you eat it. Enjoy it for me."

"Okay," he said, smiling, though he gave himself a little whisper as he took the first bite. He looked up at the stars, taking tiny bites from the cake as if he meant to make it last all night.

"Oh, there's the Mother's Home!" he cried, pointing at a constellation.

Shaped like a sort of twisted flower, its petals reached out from a central star, the entire thing formed into a cup around a patch of darkness in the center. She hadn't had much time for stars under the mask, but everyone knew that one, its name mentioned over and over in the Odes.

"Do you think that's really where the Sacred Mother came from?" he asked, leaning forward as he stared into the sky. "I mean…they're just stars. It's not like there's *places* out there, right? Or was *she* a star?"

"I…" she started. What did she believe? *Something* had happened at the temple, the whispers of the gods urging her on, giving her strength she shouldn't have had. Still, all of that was shrouded in guilt now, the power taken from her when she fled. But she found herself believing in that something, even if she didn't understand the rest.

"I'm not sure," she finally said. "Maybe it's just a story."

Was that what she should say to a boy? He slowly nodded, keeping his eyes on the stars. She squeezed him tighter, watching with him, hoping her silent presence was enough.

"What about the Day of Joy? Is that real?"

"You mean the holiday? Isn't it just their new year?"

He shook his head in the crook of her arm, taking another bite of his oat cake.

"No, it's like a legend. The Snow Father, one of their elders, brought them to this place, but it was too cold. On the Day of Loss, his wife died. They thought they'd all die too, but they did something with blood — I don't understand the Deynen for that yet — and they survived. On the Day of Joy, the snow melted, and they knew they'd live."

Eyri felt a chill, cutting deeper than just the night air. Blood magic. It was the one thing the Deynens had that the Zennans did not. The thing that almost cost them the war.

"The magic here is strange, Teros, evil even. Be careful what you read."

"But I—" he started, but she shushed him.

"Just be careful," she said, caressing his head. She didn't ever want him to know what she'd gone through in the war. Maybe he'd read about it eventually in his books, but that was different, sanitized.

She heard a whistle and looked up, finding a bright orange ball arcing into the sky. It exploded, showering the mountain in green sparks. Soon, the sky was covered in them, the fireworks from the village joining those from the city as they filled the sky. She clenched her jaw, suddenly reminded of something else from the war, the night sky filled with a different kind of fire. Still, Teros was enthralled, his eyes wide as he watched, their conversation forgotten. She clung to him, her only life raft in the night. The Day of Joy… At least one of them had found some.

5

8ᵗʰ of Selomira 979
Rule of the Vindeista
(10ᵗʰ of Perat-kam, 985, 23ʳᵈ Year of Iron)

Chir walked down the street with his head held high, the Zinc Quarter rising before him like a hungry monster. He tightened his cloak, refastening it with his guild pin, the gold brooch glowing in the morning sun as it crept above the mountains. The lesser zincsmiths stood outside their shops to watch the procession, while nearly every guild member with voting rights was on their way to watch the duels. Some raised a hand in greeting, but just as many turned to whisper, no doubt gossiping about him.

Fools, all of them. Everyone in the zinc guild pretended they believed in the system. *Strength determines rank,* they liked to say. But when someone like his grandson began the climb, they were so quick to cut him down, eager to slam the gate behind them. But didn't they feel the need for change? Had they forgotten everything the war had seared into his memory? More than half their knights had died, eleven hundred men choking on their own blood on the western flats. He'd earned his vote on the guild by holding those men's hands, repairing their swords as they rode off again and again to certain death.

Perhaps it was guilt that made them shun his grandson. Or fear, knowing their time of mismanaging the kingdom was nearly up. Sonote would fight today for his spot in the Third Zamak. After that, he would fight to become a Zinc Lord, with only three more rungs between him and the generals — and a spot on the king's council. Perhaps he would even defeat the king himself and all this foolishness would finally end.

If only there was more time. Only a fool would deny something was happening in the ranks of the Chiremir. He wasn't high enough to know all their secrets, but it didn't take a genius to know what all those new sword orders meant. And the orders for cobalt... Were those dogs really so hungry for war they'd risk making serosine again? If only Sonote could climb faster. Chir's own life was almost over, but his grandson's wasn't. And what good would it be for Sonote to survive the duels only to die in another pointless fight with Pen'dil Zenn?

Finally, he reached the stadium, the cobblestones of the street giving way to a wide square of black marble. He crossed into the stadium's shadow, like a mountain itself with its tall stone walls. Or perhaps it was more like a castle, though one where the enemies were *inside* the gates. All the guild members seemed to reach the square at the same time, the power of tradition pushing them forward like a mighty wind. Even as they'd surely gossip inside, no one looked at each other on the square, unsure of themselves until they took their seats, where rank would finally be made clear by their proximity to the king.

Chir joined the sea of bodies, flowing through the arch before they all split up, taking whichever one of the dozen flights of stairs was closest to their seats. His seat, of course, was new. After Sonote had won his last duel, the court officials had begrudgingly moved him closer to the king. Shaped like a horseshoe, he was near the center of the arena now, even if he was still seven rows below the royal box. Not that he cared for his own rank, but the closer he moved to the king, the closer he was to breaking that devil's grip on Pen'dil Deyn.

The king, Iremi nal Miri, was already there, and each person had to bow to him at the foot of the stairs — not that the king ever seemed to notice. He had a goblet in his hand, and he was talking to the pretty young consorts at his side, the queen strangely absent. At least his sword bearer was worth his metal. The king's knight stood at attention in full plate, *Eng'ideref* — the Sword of Longing — in his hands. Chir had only seen the blade freed from its bejeweled scabbard once, but it was a beauty, held by dozens of kings since the time of the Zinc Father. Perhaps when he and Sonote freed the kingdom, they would free the blade too, restoring it to its proper glory.

Still, after so much loss, so much sacrilege, it was somehow strange to think of the Zinc Father on a day like today. Was this what he'd intended for his people, fighting over scraps and scrambling for power? Everything they did in the arena was *supposedly* in his name, the rules of dueling carefully prescribed from the earliest days. They even still barred dueling on the Day of Joy, the holiday between the 7th and 8th when everyone in the city tripped over themselves to celebrate the end of winter.

But why bother pausing the duels when the Zinc Quarter barely seemed to notice the festival at all? After all, the holiday commemorated the founding of the city by the Snow Father, an Elder the king clearly thought little of now. In some ways, Pen'dil Deyn was really two kingdoms, with the waterfall dividing them like a wall made of ice. Perhaps they'd been friends once, the two founders — the Snow Father supposedly having even made the sacred sword in his own forge — but you could hardly tell now. Iremi nal Miri pretended to serve the merchant council, but it was clear he though only of his own throne — and his wars, of course.

Chir took his seat quickly, ignoring his new neighbors as he stared at the entrance to the practice room. He had seen Sonote at home, of course, but there hadn't been time to visit him before the match. So he sent him his good wishes now, praying the lad could feel his love through the stones. At that very moment — a good omen, perhaps? — his grandson appeared, walking out with the princeling he would beat, the two young men moving to the middle of the arena as they waited for the bout to begin.

As the last guild voter took his seat, they slowly lowered the stadium's gate, the horseshoe becoming a circle as the exit was sealed. The flat stone of the arena was filled with glittering metal windmills, their fans slowly spinning in the wind from the mountains. With the pull of a lever, the walls groaned, sealing off the audience as giant spikes extended on springs every few feet along the perimeter. Their rusted iron spread out like porcupine quills, leaving very little space between them.

The boys slowly moved apart from each other, with Sonote, as challenger, taking the east side beneath the king. The crown squire stepped forward from the king's box, a scroll in his hand.

"On this day, the 8th of Selomira, one sunrise after the Day of Joy as prescribed by law, Sonote nir Chiremir, grandson of guild voter Chir nir Chiremir, has challenged Lonfan nir Stal for his rank in the Third Zamak."

Chir stood at the mention of his name, putting a fist to his chest. Let the others stare; he stood with his grandson. Even he — Chir nir Chiremir — with his peasant's name, had risen high enough to challenge those in power. The rich all named their children for precious gems or for great knights from the stories. His had only known to name him after the blade itself, the precious zinc of the gods they prayed to. They'd hoped desperately he might learn to read the wind and become a knight, but despite all their sacrifices, he'd only ever made it to the rank of squire.

Still, he'd given everything to this kingdom. He'd lost a pinky in the mountains, desperate to pass the winter trials and join the army. He'd helped bury the dead at Cs'ira Hill during the war, melting down their swords to make new blades. He'd even given his own son on the Day of the Hawk, a common soldier run through by one of the masked devils from Zenn. All of it sacrificed for a meaningless war. But now, the gods had finally answered. All the power he'd never had had been heaped on his grandson's head, and they would use it to fight.

Sonote stepped forward, pulling his sword from its hilt. It was hard to feel anything beyond the tension in his chest, but there was a flutter of pride as the stadium filled with whispers. Barely half this number had attended his grandson's last duel, but word of his sword — and how fiercely he fought with it — had clearly spread. Chir had made it himself, spending an entire month with his face in the forge, and there was no other like it.

Vandraeb, the *Killer of Winds.* Like all zinc swords, it was as long as Sonote's arm, but its blade was split, a notch running three quarters of the way toward the hilt. Each tong of the forked blade had a different amalgam — mercury to match his enemy's wind and silver to redirect it. In short, it was his vengeance.

A sword made to kill zinc knights rather than defend them. Most duels involved the princelings trading gales until one of them ended up pinned against the wall, yielding before his foe could push him into the spikes and end his privileged little life — after all, even a cast down lord was still richer than the gods. But not Sonote. His grandson fought to kill.

The young men — boys, really, compared to Chir — put their swords in the air, and the squire called for the duel to begin. Chir sat, his hands making fists against his robes. The breeze he had felt from the mountains disappeared, the pressure in the arena growing as the boys summoned Identity. Even if he couldn't read the winds himself, you'd be a fool not to feel it.

So much power. These lads, young as they were, called upon the gods themselves, the mighty storms of Sen'el'seng rushing to aid them in their battle. If only that were enough. Like so many others in this basin, he'd thought zinc knights impossible to defeat once. After all, what could slay a god? But he'd been shown otherwise. Those masked demons from Zenn had shown him the truth, the *anndem* with no souls of their own.

The windmills started spinning faster, currents forming in the arena as Lonfan prepared his gales. But not Sonote. He was prepared for a different fight entirely.

Lonfan lashed out, slicing through the air with his sword as a burst of wind leapt from his blade. It was visible now, rushing through the windmills and kicking up dust from the stone. It shot at Sonote with a terrible hiss. But just as it was about to strike, his grandson whipped his own sword through the air, deflecting the other man's wind. Sonote spun, sending the broken gale back around the sides of the arena where it smashed into Lonfan like a clap of thunder.

Suddenly Sonote moved, dashing between the spinning windmills as Lonfan scrambled to his feet. The princeling swung in a wide, desperate arc, launching another wave of wind, but Sonote was ready. He swung upward with his forked blade, cleaving the wind in two as it crashed into the crowd, pulling at their robes. There was an audible gasp at that, the new audience still unprepared for Sonote's style. Surprise served the boy now, but what of his next battle? After the Third Zamak, the fights would almost certainly get harder. The real question was: would the zinc lords change their strategy to beat him or cling to the old ways?

It mattered little today. There was a look of shock on Lonfan's face as Sonote reached him, as if he hadn't thought it possible. He was still in the past when zinc knights never struck each other. He was so surprised, he barely got his sword up as Sonote swung, their blades meeting with a clang that sent Lonfan to his knees again. Before he could get up, Sonote kicked him in his chest plate, crashing him against the wall. The princeling flailed against the wood, trying to get up without spearing himself on the rusted spikes. But Sonote had finally summoned his own Identity, pinning Lonfan with a powerful gale.

"Do you yield?!" Sonote shouted above the howling wind.

Lonfan looked out into the crowd, fear in his eyes. He was looking for his father, Lord General Stal sitting just one row below the king. The man stood silently, his gaze piercing as he looked down upon his struggling son. It was a rebuke. His son could die, but Lord Stal would never let him yield.

"No!" Lonfan yelled back, his voice full of fear. But he still couldn't stand, couldn't fight against the wind. Perhaps they thought Sonote would agree to a draw? After all, it had been years since actual blood was shed in the arena, since the king's own grab for power. Sonote had drawn plenty of blood in his other duels, but the little rich boys had been smart enough to yield before the end.

It was Sonote's turn to look through the crowd, his eyes wide as he searched for his grandfather. Chir stood, staring back as their eyes met.

"Do it," he mouthed, nodding to his grandson. It was hard, yes, but so was climbing any mountain. They had discussed the cost, and Sonote had agreed. But was he ready? The boy hadn't seen what Chir had seen, had been a mere boy when the war ended. Sonote felt plenty of rage for his family, true, for all his mother's sobs at night, but would that be enough to make him kill? To avenge a father he could hardly remember?

Sonote moved slowly, like a man caught in a dream, his sword trailing behind him as he walked toward the princeling.

"No, please, no," Lonfan cried, shuffling like a crab as he tried to disappear into the wood. Sonote dropped his wind, allowing the other boy to stand. Still, he had lost his sword long ago, the blade forgotten on the stone just out of reach.

"Do you yield?" Sonote asked again, his voice barely audible even in the silence of the windless arena.

Lonfan licked his lips, flexing his hands at his sides.

"Never!" he suddenly cried out, his voice shrill from fear.

Lonfan dashed for his sword, sliding to the ground as he reached his blade. It was a credit to Sonote he even let the princeling touch the hilt. But as merciful as his grandson was, he was no fool either. In the arena, you either finished things or had them finished for you.

Lonfan tried to come up in a swing, but Sonote had found his throat, his blade darting like a serpent's tongue between the gaps in his armor. Like a flame, the sword flickered back out just as quickly, the duel complete. Blood sprayed from the princeling's neck, and the boy fell to his knees for the last time, the arena stunned into silence.

"The…the duel goes to Sonote nir Chiremir," the squire said as he hastily stood. "Lord General Ondcat nir Stal and guild voter Chir nir Chiremir will stand as required by the law."

Neither of the men had sat back down, of course, frozen as they watched the fight play out, but they turned toward each other. Stal was an evil man, a man who had ordered thousands of deaths, but the general looked…destroyed. *Steel yourself,* Chir thought as both men bowed — his a little lower as he gave the boy's father his due respect. *Don't grow soft now.*

They were walking the mountain of death, where the roads were paved with bones. Still, he felt a flash of fear. Would there ever be a day when he risked as much? When he lost his grandson for the cause?

Finally, the crowd began to cheer, though it was a spiritless thing. They cheered because they were supposed to. Just like the men bowing to each other, the guild — the *system* — came first. But if that system was a ladder, they would climb it to the king and topple his crown. But all of that could wait. Now, he had to find Sonote.

Fighting his way through the crowd — and a handful of begrudging congratulations — Chir made it to the practice room. Lord Stal's guards were already there, but even as they glared, they decided to let him in. Apparently, some traditions were too sacred to ignore. Even if he himself was a prisoner to the tradition he must face next…

Inside, there were two golden altars, the metal glowing dully in the torch light. Sonote sat on one, his face blank as he stared. On the other, covered in gold cloth, was the body of Lonfan, Lord Stal praying quietly at his side. *This* was the real cost of what they did. However repugnant the generals were, this man had lost a son. Chir bowed before the dead boy, forcing himself to whisper a prayer.

"Sonote," he said to his grandson, the boy blinking in surprise as if he'd only just noticed him.

"There was so much blood," Sonote said quietly, his eyes never leaving the other altar. "They just kept mopping it up; they wouldn't even let Lord Stal in at first."

"It's alright," Chir said, sitting beside him. *Vandraeb* was back in its sheath, Sonote's hand squeezing the hilt, his gauntlets forgotten at his side.

"I did that," Sonote whispered. "I…can't believe I did that."

Chir took a bloody cloth from his pocket, tying it around the boy's hilt before he could think too much about it. The blood was faded, more rust than red now, but he had kept it for himself for long enough.

"Remember why we fight," he said, taking his grandson firmly by the shoulder. "This is your father's blood, boy, spilled by their hands. Your mother's tears, shed for their wickedness. You have to fight, and you have to *win*. We can count our losses when we're finished."

Sonote finally looked at him, his eyes searching like a man who'd forgotten his own guild. Finally, he nodded, even as he withdrew further into himself, the boy in him disappearing before the man could arrive.

"We fight on," he said, pulling his grandson close. Even as he felt the boy's tears start against his robe — even as he blamed himself for this boy's pain — he knew they had no choice. They had begun their path, and slowing would only give their enemies a chance. For now, they had to fight on. They had to pray that was enough.

6

9th of Selomira 979
Rule of the Vindeista
(11th of Perat-kam, 985, 23rd Year of Iron)

As Eyri climbed the road up into the city, the traffic grew, the hill serving as a chokepoint for all the farmers and yak herders heading into town. It was always busy on the road from the southern flats, of course, but this had to be some kind of post-holiday rush. After all of Deyn had stopped working for the Day of Joy, they all seemed desperate to get their business done now.

Still, it always surprised her just how *big* the kingdom was, like a city in reverse, how many people it held outside its boundaries. After all, the fields here were *outside* of town, not at all like the royal gardens she'd known her whole life. Even stranger was the city itself, cascading ever downwards from the mountain and its ice shelf down into the first city, the waterfall, and the Zinc Quarter below. Couldn't anything in Deyn just be flat?

A farmer passed, somehow out-walking her despite the pole over his back, weighed down by thick woven baskets on either side. Despite his obvious labor, though, he was dressed in a colorful tunic, just like everyone else she'd passed so far today. It seemed they'd all taken out their best clothes for the holiday and were loath to take them off. She, for one, was glad the holiday was over. Teros, of course, had been thrilled to watch the fireworks. At least she'd given him something of a holiday, but after spending the 8th of Selomira hauling manure on the farms, she needed real work again.

As she reached the top of the incline, it put her at the perfect angle to see the ice shelf. Looming above the city, it was perfectly blue. She could still remember looking up at it during the war the day they'd destroyed the dam, but that felt so far away now. With all the merchants rushing about, crossing over the surging black river, it felt like she'd dreamt the war entirely.

She paused for a moment at the bridge — getting out of the way of a particularly ornery yak herder, which at least gave her time to look at the statues. Forged into the ice itself, the largest was of a woman, her face full of tears as she looked toward Sen'el'tul, her hair like a second river. Was that the Snow Father's wife Teros had mentioned? The ice had finally melted past her feet, receding up the shelf. Was that how they knew it was time for the holiday? It seemed like Deyn was a never-ending series of holidays — a string of days she'd no doubt go hungry when she couldn't find work.

As she finally crossed the river, it felt like the holiday hadn't really ended. There were still streamers littering the street, with more than a few stuck to the buildings as shop boys scrambled up ladders to pull them down. Even with all her sweeping on the holiday, the refuse seemed infinite. Perhaps that was why they celebrated so close to the New Year, so they could spend the other ten months cleaning up after the parades.

She started in the First Ward, the giant ovens of the Bake D'iyl seeming to push back the lingering cold of winter. She didn't much like the Baker's Guild — a standoffish bunch if she'd ever met one — but it was the first guild district over the bridge, and with Baker's Day at the end of Selomira, they should at least have work. There was always a risk of getting paid in bread, but there had to be someone willing to pay a few siulkiy to move some boxes.

She started on the street with all the bakeries, the signs shaped like bread or cake or *ka'pon* at least giving her some clue of what they sold when she didn't know the words in Deynen. The buildings were like castles, made of real stone blocks — no doubt dug from the mountain quarries — but each shop had an open half wall where the shopkeeper could sell to people on the street. They hated when you came up to the window without buying anything, of course, but she'd also learned the hard way how the ones with guards treated people coming through the door without an invitation.

So, she began her awkward dance, sidling up to the windows trying to catch each shopkeeper's eye while staying in the corner so she wouldn't block their customers. The groveling certainly hadn't come naturally — not after two decades behind the mask — but she would do it if it meant feeding Teros. The first was a stout man, one she hadn't tried before, and she found him approaching the window with two huge trays of pastries in his hands. Like every bloody person in Deyn, he eyed her left breast where a guild pin should have been, raising his eyebrows.

"Cun'fael," he said, giving her a slight nod as he put down his trays, leaving his right hand cupped around his own sparkling guild pin. *Cun'fael* meant cousin or something, implying she wasn't of his guild. *"Tej'ser lin mil'stey?"*

At least she could understand more than she could speak — Teros's exasperated nightly lessons notwithstanding. But it was a standard greeting, 'how may I serve,' as if the Deynens weren't as bloodthirsty as every other kingdom in the valley. Still, she could only respond with a single useless word in her broken accent.

"Arb'voro," she said, not even managing to make it a question. *"Arb'voro siulkiy."* *Work for money.*

The man sighed, suddenly looking far older as he wiped his brow. He sized her up again as he slowly shook his head. Still, he fumbled around some drawers, finally handing her a sealed parchment scroll. He leaned out the window, pointing down the street where a hawk messenger's stand was.

"Besk'e lif spar'fa, eh?" he said, pointing again. He picked up one of his pastries, showing it to her. *"Besk'e lif spar'fa."*

She thought about taking the pastry, showing just how far she'd fallen, but it was hardly a reasonable payment for just delivering a message. Besides, it would be crushed in her pocket by the end of the day when she reached Teros. More importantly, she had to have some dignity left, something of her own to offer. This was clearly a good man, kinder than most simply by choosing not to curse her or spit in her face.

"Dey'n'lof, cun'fael," she said, thanking him as she nodded. She waved off the pastry, raising the scroll as she walked toward the hawk messenger.

"Dey'n'lof!" he called after her.

The hawk messenger gave her a look — though he couldn't refuse a scroll with a guild seal on it — and she started the process again at the next shop window. Unfortunately, by the time she reached the other end of the guild district, she had nothing to show for herself but a small bag of grain she'd earned sweeping out an alley. She finally took a break in the central square, the one place too sacred for the guards to kick you out for sitting. Not that it was a particularly relaxing place…

Sitting in the square put her face to face with the city's sacred tower, a sort of Deynen temple — and the only place in the city that could make her feel even more useless than she already did. Like a bright white knife against the dark stone of the mountains, the tower stood just behind Deyn's two pillars. They weren't carved into the shape of the Elders like the ones back home, but it was a reminder all the same. She had no magic now. She was useless; a nobody, not even able to get a job at a bakery.

Her first week in the city, she'd tried getting close to the pillars, even if only to hear their whispers again. But even now, she could see the shine of armor, a knight and three guards patrolling the perimeter. The one who'd caught her touching the pillar hadn't been gentle, the bruises lasting over a month on her meager diet, even with Teros forcing his mountain herbs on her every night.

Still, sitting there wasn't completely without its pleasures. The city was always warmer than the mountains — warming cobalt pillars could be found on every corner — and sitting in the sun, it felt almost like being back in Zenn. She pulled off her cloak, draping it over her knees as she closed her eyes, tilting her face toward the light. She missed home. It was strange to admit that to herself after so many years of pining for this place, for the death she'd promised herself at the foot of Sen'el'tul. But beyond wanting redemption, beyond feeling the same loyalty — however misguided — she really, truly *missed* Pen'dil Zenn. The river, the Wist Ristare, even the Stone Districts. The city was a part of her.

"Far from home?" a voice asked in Zennan.

Eyri jerked awake, her hand reaching for a sword she wasn't wearing. She blinked in the light, finding an old priest beside her. He had white hair, which seemed almost ghostly against the black of his priest's robes. She stood to go, but he gently took her shoulder.

"It's alright," he said. "I mean no harm. I've just done some traveling. You're Zennan, no?"

Her mind whirred. It was unlikely the Deynens would cooperate with her crown, but she was still a wanted woman, and there would no doubt be a ransom. Still, it wasn't like she was the only woman from Zenn in the whole basin.

"No," she mumbled. "Or…yes. You're not wrong. I'm just late for work. Excuse me."

"I understand," he said, smiling. He only had a few teeth left, but the ones he had were surprisingly bright. "Still, perhaps you'll humor me. If all we do is work, there's no room for the gods."

She glanced at the pillars as she nodded, slipping from his grip as she backed away a step. She'd heard of the priests of Deyn, of course. They had their own guild, but they supposedly spent all their time in the mountains "seeking the gods." And when they weren't climbing through frozen passages to their secret hot springs, they were obsessed with coercing regular people into taking their advice.

"I suppose you're right," she said, "but I'm alright, really."

The priest reached in his pocket, pulling out an orange. Suddenly, she couldn't help herself. She stared at it, immediately imagining what it would taste like. She hadn't seen fruit — *real* fruit — in months. Only the priests with their hidden groves could grow things like that in Deyn, and she would certainly never earn enough to buy one on her own.

"See?" he asked, gesturing for her to take it. "The gods aren't heartless."

She took it despite herself, tucking it into her robes before he could change his mind. Still, her neck burned with shame, sure she'd regret giving him an opening.

"Now, tell me, what is your purpose? I see you have no guild pin, but do you feel a certain…*task* the gods have set out for you? Something only you can do? Surely you had your reasons to move to a different kingdom — especially one as cold as this — but I sense a…doubt about you. You see, a priest's job is to help others seek their call, to find their purpose."

"I have a child," she said. "And all I want is to feed him. Perhaps the gods will find *his* purpose worthy." She glanced at the crowds around them, but no one seemed to be watching. At least a priest cornering someone was normal, even if it felt like the farthest thing from it to her.

"Motherhood is a noble thing," he said, nodding. "But it doesn't preclude your own call. As the Snow Father once said, constellations tells stories, but they do so *through* each star."

She bit her lip. What was she supposed to say? She needed work, but she had no guild affiliation. Could this man help her? Unfortunately, her time as a Masked One hadn't taught her how to convince people, only to wield authority.

"I have no guild home," she said, trying to say it how the locals did. "Perhaps…you could find me work? I think my calling will be clearer with a full belly."

The priest laughed, nodding.

"A valid argument. Like the Snow Father once said, 'only with a warm fire can we dream of spring.' Go to the docks and ask for a merchant named F'iyn. Tell him So'rek sent you. Perhaps you'll find your purpose there."

And with that, the priest disappeared into the crowd. Without meaning to, she lowered herself to the curb again, staring at the orange in her hand. She felt a jolt of happiness, thinking of giving it to Teros later, but she felt…confused, too. Was she really meant to find her purpose here? She looked at the pillars again, the faces of the gods who mocked her. She thought suddenly of one of the Wise Father's poems.

"Free me from the binds of life, so I can walk the only path worth walking. The path of the other, the path of service."

The binds of life… Had Entodal nol Serimh, with all his magic, really felt trapped, *bound* by life? She knew *she* did, impossibly so. She needed to care for Teros, and that meant working from sunup to sundown without ever getting ahead. And yet, she'd felt a glimmer of the gods. Fighting in the temple that day, she'd felt…*something,* something impossibly real and true. *Save him. Save Borash.* It had been a call to be free, to be the little girl they'd stolen from her. That single thought had been enough to conquer armies — if only for a moment. But what was she now? A joke. Less than a worm to the knights of this city, walking no path at all.

"Free me from the binds of life," she begged the pillars. Even knowing they couldn't hear her, would maybe never whisper to her again. "Just show me how to be *something* again."

7

9ᵗʰ of Selomira 979
Rule of the Vindeista
(11ᵗʰ of Perat-kam, 985, 23ʳᵈ Year of Iron)

Teros looked up from his book, eyeing the pile of herbs at his feet. He had spent the morning collecting them, sneaking through the mountain passes. Oddly, even at this elevation, there were many of the same ones Mother had taught him about on the farm. He actually smiled thinking of her, remembering the rare days they'd had to themselves when Uncle Elin was away in the city. It was getting easier to focus on Mother's good face, he just needed a happy memory to use. Even if other faces were bringing him more pain these days…

He picked up one of the herbs, rolling it in his hand. The bags under Eyri's eyes were getting worse. She was working much too hard, and he could tell she wasn't eating enough. Herbs were supposed to be powerfully magical foods, but so far, all of his tinctures had failed to bring her strength back. It had to be the water. The water they had was delicious — made from boiled snow filtered by the mountains — but it lacked *power.* It wasn't from the sacred river, wasn't fed by Sen'el'seng and the gods. But the village, Hv'rano, had a well…

He got up, reaching for their canteen when he froze, an image of Eyri scolding him appearing in his mind. He shook his head. *No.* He was doing this for her. He shut his eyes, whispering his new lucky words to himself.

"Together, together, together."

It had taken him a lot to get Mother's voice out of his head, telling him to be free. Even if he *was* free now, thinking about it only brought back the guilt — Borash, the temple, all the things he couldn't change. But he *could* change this. He had been practicing his Deynen, and Hv'rano was just over the next ridge. He couldn't bring back Borash, but he could help his sister, and if he kept Eyri healthy, then they could stay together, they could stay safe.

"Together," he said more loudly, forcing himself to walk toward the hole in the chasm.

Besides, he wouldn't mind a chance to speak Deynen after all his studying, even if it was only to make sure his voice was still there. It had been getting harder to speak lately, the thoughts in his head piling up in his throat like stones. Even with Eyri — not that he had anyone else to talk to — he had to think his words twice before he could say them, trying to follow them with his mouth as quickly as he could before they disappeared. But maybe Deynen would be different. If he had to spend all his time thinking about what the words *were,* they couldn't possibly get stuck in his mouth, right?

He left the chasm, leaving the moss perfectly placed over the door. Eyri was almost never home early, especially lately, but she would be cross if he didn't hide their home properly. Not that the moss would save him from her moods if she caught him sneaking off… But what was the harm? She didn't have to know he went to the village. He could always say he'd been hiking the yak trails.

He stopped, squeezing his eyes shut. *No.* That would be a lie.

"Together, together, together," he whispered.

He couldn't lie to Eyri. There had been enough lies in Zenn to last a lifetime. They had to be different now. If he started lying, he wouldn't be any different than the Masked Ones. Even if she was cross with him, he loved Eyri, and you didn't lie to people you loved, right?

Teros continued down the valley, sticking to the shadows how Eyri had taught him. He looked up at the sky as he walked, the deep blue like a river in reverse as it traced the dark stone of the mountains. But the sky was so *much* bluer in Deyn. Why was that? Was it the mountains? He'd never thought the sky could be different. After all, they'd only traveled a hundred miles.

He passed a patch of moss and picked it up, slowly pulling it apart as he walked. He was slowly learning how to turn it into thread, which he could use to fix Eyri's cloak. It had been cheap when she'd bought it, and it was starting to get holes in a few places, especially along the edges. Though he'd still need a good needle to do anything truly useful. Could he get one in town? He'd need to trade for it, of course — or else find work like Eyri did — but if Hv'rano had a tailor, he could probably work something out.

Thoughts like those — and seemingly a million of them — kept his mind so busy, he almost didn't notice when he reached the end of the valley. Suddenly, the mountain pass fell away, and the southern flats were just…there. He stopped, staring. He'd seen Deyn from the mountains plenty of times, of course, but this was the first time he'd left the valley since they'd arrived. From here, it felt impossibly huge, like it could swallow him whole.

He took a deep breath, closing his eyes as he took his first step away from the mountains.

"Together, together, together."

———

Eyri picked up two more bags of flour, gritting her teeth to keep from wincing. This had to be the hundredth pair she'd carried, but she couldn't afford to stop moving. After trying a dozen of her usual places to no avail, she'd been forced to accept a job from a new man. She didn't like it — hated being forced to trust strangers, actually — but it was better than going hungry.

"Me'gtahn lif tashtara, cun'fael," the foreman said, chuckling as he walked by, his "watch" in his hand. As if it were normal for a man to have his own clock in any place but Deyn!

The other sailors laughed, too — albeit quietly — even as their heads never lifted from their own work. She didn't understand the whole sentence, but she knew his meaning well enough — there were a lot of bags left in her pile, and she was running out of time. When she'd asked for work, he'd pointed to the pile of flour before pointing at the larger clock on the docks. She had until the fifth bell to put every sack in a cart. Even if she succeeded, he'd probably stiff her, but what choice did she have?

Her legs shook as she walked down the plank, adding the flour to the cart with a thud. She forced herself to jog back to the boat, draping a sack over her neck so she could try taking three at a time. Was the captain using her for sport? The men at the docks were always in a hurry, true, but if this shipment was for an important customer, why weren't the others helping? She'd probably regret it in the morning, though that was assuming she'd have the strength to walk home when she was done…

By some miracle, she finished before the bell, though she almost didn't believe it herself at first. She stood at the edge of the ship where the pile used to be, looking down at it in a trance. Then, without meaning to, she fell to a seat, exhaustion filling every inch of her. She could just see over the edge of the barge, and she watched the black water slipping by, reflecting the sky back at her like some dark and twisted mirror. Was the water this black back home? The river certainly wasn't clear in Zenn, but with it only spending a hundred yards in the sunlight there, it didn't seem *this* black, like liquid midnight. Of course, she hadn't really had time to think about it until she left. She—

"Hey, foreigner," one of the sailors said in Zennan, his accent thick. He was staring at her hard, one hand pointed at the clock, which was just minutes away from the fifth bell. "Boss find else no payment, yeah?"

She nodded slowly, even her chin somehow exhausted.

"Dey'n'lof," she somehow managed, pushing herself to her feet.

She looked for the boss, finding him at the next ship down on the dock, talking to another captain. He would be angry if she interrupted him, but even if it burned a bridge, it was likely the only way she'd be paid at all. They were all petty, but the captains seemed proud too, and he wouldn't skip paying her in front of his friend.

She forced her legs forward, pushing through the ache toward the two men. As she came down the plank for the last time, she eyed the clock, finding just one minute left. She hurried her step but almost ran into a cart, the driver raising his whip as he cursed at her, forcing her back against the ship. Where was he going in such a hurry? The cart was heading to the south, in the direction of the zinc knights, the royal crest printed on the cloth covering the cargo.

She stared blankly, watching it pass as she wondered what could be so important. There was a gap at the back of the cart where the cloth had stretched into an opening. It held a silvery metal, stacked in large ingots as it glittered in the sun, tiny rainbows showing up along the edges. It—

Serosine.

There was no metal like it — and none she'd been forced to know so well. On shields, in swords, through the necks of friends. It had been everything in the war, right up until she'd helped the others melt it down on the plains outside Deyn, bubbling until it turned black. She'd known it even in the hands of that man from the warehouses, Maegin. Especially then. And seeing it here meant everything she'd feared was true — the metal was back. And who else could make it but the Deynens? Who else would hide it under their royal sigil?

She turned toward the mountains, suddenly no longer tired. She needed to find Teros. They needed to do something.

"Cun'fael!" the captain yelled after her. *"Lif tashtara siul'sho!"*

But who could care about money with a sword dangling above their head? Even if she was too tired to jog, she kept walking, feeling the eyes of the sailors on her as she left the docks. Perhaps the gods had answered. She would be someone again. Someone who could save her people.

———

Teros walked toward Hv'rano on the main road, the sun actually warming his face now that he was out of the mountains. For a while, the road was hardly different from the stone around him, cut hastily from the hillside with no bricks to pave it. As he got closer to the village, though, the land began to open up, and eventually, the road cut through a huge field of tall, brown grass, the fronds waving in the wind.

He stopped, looking out at the farms as they stretched to the west. He could see people working, cutting the grass as their scythes glinted in the sun. Beyond the grass were endless fields of wheat, the golden stalks dotted with the short winter wheat they'd planted in the fall. It was a beautiful place, just like Uncle Elin's farm, the fields like the oceans of legend from the Odes — only made of gold.

Except this wasn't his uncle's pond. It was a new place, and it was full of new people, new *possibilities*. Eyri said Hv'rano had a thousand people at least, and he could see dozens of buildings. There were tall stone structures around a central square, and little houses dotting the southern hills beyond. They even had windmills, the sails spinning in the breeze.

He eyed the sun. It was still well over the western flats, giving him plenty of time to get back before Eyri came home. Maybe he could surprise her with something special for dinner? Something to show her these people were okay — assuming he left out any details that might scare her. But she clearly had nothing to worry about. How could a place this beautiful be dangerous?

He continued through the fields, passing a pair of those giant cobalt spikes marking the edge of town. Built like giant swords with the blades facing up, they radiated heat. His book said they pulled the cold from the ground, a creation of the Deynens to make this place more livable. He was tempted to touch them, but what if they were sacred? Not to mention the risk of burning his hand…

He continued into town until he reached a giant fountain. It had a stone statue in the middle, but he didn't have time to look at it as his eyes were drawn to the square around him. He was surrounded by children, dozens of them. They were of all ages, but they had spread themselves out on the cobblestones of the square where they were working, sorting brown grass the men had cut in the fields. The girl nearest to him looked up. She was about his age, but she was very pretty, her hair done up in looping braids.

"Spo'gimes?" she asked, her eyes wide.

Teros looked behind him, thinking there must be someone else. The word meant…ghost, didn't it? Did she mean him? He pointed to his chest as the girl tapped a smaller boy beside her.

"Jer'tam im spo'gimes!" she said, but she sounded excited now, not at all the voice of someone who'd seen a ghost. She waved him over, gesturing for him to sit.

"You…think I'm a ghost?" he asked in Deynen, putting the words together backwards like his book had taught him. But maybe he'd made a mistake because the girl started nodding excitedly.

"Everyone's seen you," she said, pointing in the direction of his and Eyri's hiding place up in the mountains. "I told my brother you must be a *lof'gime,* a spirit without a guild, destined to haunt the hills until you find your purpose."

Her eyes shone as she looked at the mountains, clearly enjoying this. But then she looked at him again, frowning.

"But you don't look like a ghost," she said, poking him in the shoulder. "And you don't feel like one either."

"You don't know what a ghost feels like," her brother said.

"Do too," she said, sticking her tongue out at him.

"Well, Mehm told you to stop telling scary stories. I need my sleep."

"I'm not a ghost," Teros said. But what was he? He couldn't say the truth, Eyri was right about that much. They'd agreed on a lie in case they were ever found, but would these people believe him? He also had to lie in another language when it was taking everything he had just to understand what they were saying. "I just live in the mountains with my mother. She sells rocks. We're…looking for something."

"Ah," the girl said, nodding as if she'd known this all along. "That makes more sense. You're *pec'torih,* right? People who look for fancy stones?"

He hadn't remembered the word for stones until she said it, but that sounded good. Better than *rocks.*

"Right," he said.

"And you're from Zenn?" she asked, circling her finger around her face.

"You can tell?" Teros asked.

"Sure. My Peppin sells wheat to a man from Zenn. He came here once, looks just like you."

"You don't remember," her brother said, going back to his basket. "That was years ago."

"Ignore my brother, Si'tar," the girl said. "He's a *fireplace boy.*"

Teros didn't know what that meant, but maybe it was like a momma's boy? Si'tar stuck his tongue out, so it certainly wasn't a compliment.

"Oh," the girl said, dropping her grass. She put a hand over her chest, bowing as she covered the guild emblem stitched into her shirt. "Sorry for being rude. I'm Liska."

"Teros," he said, bowing in return, even if he had no guild pin or stitching to cover with his hand.

"Here," she said, running to the pile of grass beside the fountain where she grabbed a bunch and dropped it in front of him. "You can sort these. Put them in groups by length and color. If the grownups see you doing nothing, they'll be angry. But you should come here more if your mother doesn't need you. I know they say we're *dodvris* in the city, but we have a school and everything."

He sat, trying to follow Liska's motions as she sorted her much larger pile of grass. It took him a long time to see any sort of difference between the different types, but she didn't seem to mind, smiling at him whenever their eyes met — and only occasionally pausing her own work to fix his. Besides, it was nice just sitting there, the warmth from the cobalt spikes and the sun making him feel better than he had in months.

He looked over his shoulder at the mountains in the west, trying to judge how far away the sun was from the distant peaks. It was so much harder to tell the time without meal bells, but he must have at least two hours before Eyri was home. Maybe they'd let him take some grass home to give to her? It wouldn't be easy to tell her he'd been in the village, but she had to see that this was a good thing, right? These people were kind, and they didn't even mind that he was Zennan. It was just grass, but maybe it would prove to her he could spend time here without putting them in danger.

"What is all this grass for?" he asked Liska, finally finishing his first pile and grabbing another.

"Baker's Day," she said, frowning. "It's the end of Selomira. You don't have that in Zenn?"

He shook his head though he understood, thinking back to his book. The *Laugda im Lofre* marked every month with a special day for one of the ten guilds.

"But isn't that for the bakers, the…*Selnani?*" he asked, pointing at the guild emblem on her chest. "Aren't you in the Farmer's Guild?"

"Of course," she said, laughing. "Only fools aren't *Si'talisk,* but who do you think sells the bakers all their grain? We mill all the winter grain right before the holiday and they sell the extra bread in our baskets. You can't really have any holiday without the farms."

"Not if you're a zinc knight," Si'tar said. "Their holiday doesn't use food."

"Fa'nc," Liska said sharply, bopping him on the head.

He balled up his fists, looking like he was ready to *fight,* when a door opened on the other side of the square.

Two women walked out carrying big trays of bread. There was so much, Teros thought it might be a bakery, but a sign next to the door said it was the Guild House, *Laugda ir Forsari.* The bread was darker than the loaves Eyri had brought home from the city, the winter wheat making it a rustic brown. Setting the bread down on benches, the adults gestured for the children to take it. They all seemed to run up at once, every pile of grass abandoned for the moment.

"Come on," Liska said, offering her hand as she pulled him up. They entered the scrum, Liska the first to push to the front, returning with three large rolls. She handed the biggest one to her brother, rubbing his head.

"Don't be mad," she said, laughing, and Si'tar laughed too, tearing his roll in two. She handed another to Teros, nodding toward their spot back on the stones.

He sat again, trying to copy them as he tore his roll in half, scooping out the soft inside. It was still warm, fresh from the oven, and it smelled amazing. Uncle Elin had grown winter wheat too, but this didn't look like any bread he'd ever had in Zenn. Did they grow a different kind here? It certainly couldn't have been any wheat he'd had before, the Passing making even the simplest bread back home smell disgusting.

He popped the bread in his mouth, shutting his eyes as he savored it. It was…incredible. Filled with some kind of herb, it was still sweet somehow. When he opened his eyes, Liska was laughing at him.

"You like it?"

He nodded. "It's really good. How do you make it?"

"Guild secret," she said, tapping her emblem with two fingers. "But there's honey on the top."

He looked again at the shell he'd broken in half, the top glazed an amber color.

"Thanks for letting me have some," he said, pulling off a piece of the shell and pushing it into his cheek to melt the glaze.

"Thank you for helping. We live by the Snow Father here. Every hand works, every hand eats."

"What—" he started, when he froze.

"Teros," a familiar voice hissed, sending a chill up his spine.

He turned, finding Eyri at the edge of the square, her eyes ablaze.

He immediately stood, leaving his bread and basket on the ground.

"Come," she said, pointing beside her.

Liska stood too, bowing with her hand on her guild patch.

"Your son was helping us, ma'am. He was very good."

Eyri frowned, clearly not understanding the Deynen. The door to the guild house opened again, the adults looking out at Eyri, concerned.

"Sculdyi," she said in a thick accent. *Sorry.* "Let's go," she said to Teros, turning back toward the mountains.

He looked back at Liska one last time, waving in apology as he scurried behind her, suddenly feeling very cold as they went into the mountains, leaving the warmth of the village behind.

8

9th of Selomira 979
Rule of the Vindeista
(11th of Perat-kam, 985, 23rd Year of Iron)

Eyri stalked across the stones of the yak trail, Teros following behind her. Her head was a swirl of emotions, her shoulder knotting like it used to at the tower. She was impossibly angry, as if she'd burned Passion, the Passing searing through her veins. She'd been terrified when she rushed home to find Teros missing. She'd found the strength to run through her exhaustion then, sprinting back down the mountain where she'd found a tiny boot print in a patch of moss. Still, she'd thought he must have been taken, the print left on purpose to tell her which direction he'd been taken.

She ground her teeth. Of all the damnable things to feel, she felt *ashamed* somehow too. The look of terror on his face, those people in the village staring at her... Was this how mothers felt? Her anger, at least, was self-righteous, white-hot and poured out for his sake, but she couldn't shake the feeling she was doing everything wrong too. All those guild workers in their perfect green tunics, staring at the cheap white rags they'd sold her when she first arrived.

They passed the patch of moss where Teros had left his boot print, and she stooped down, fixing it.

"This is why we keep to the stones," she spat, meeting his eyes.

He nodded his head, looking away. She saw herself through his eyes for a moment, a monster, a thing of terror, but he *needed* to know things like this. He needed to be safe. There could be a bounty, a price on their heads, he—

She heard a shriek overhead, a hawk passing the valley on its way to the city. Her heart pounded, another memory of the war forcing its way into her mind.

"We have to hurry," she said, grabbing Teros by the sleeve. "We need to find a new cave. The hawks go straight to the zinc knights. They know who we are, we—"

"They *don't*," Teros said, his face tight as he met her eyes. He suddenly seemed much older. He squeezed her hand, slowly taking it from his shoulder.

39

"I know you're scared, and I'm sorry I broke the rules, but we have to meet these people. They already know we're here anyway. They call us *spo'gimes,* ghosts, and if they wanted to report us, they would have done it months ago. We'll be safer if they learn to trust us. I could approach them for you. I could even…go to their school."

She followed the hawk with her eyes, its shape growing smaller as it disappeared over the next ridge. He was right, of course. After all, she'd sent a message for that baker via hawk that morning. There was no war, no scouts watching from the hills. She wasn't just a terrible mother to Teros, she was a fool too, thinking herself invisible as she tried to hide them in the mountains. She pinched the bridge of her nose, taking a deep breath.

"You're sure?"

"Yes," he said. "They're nice. I could speak to them in Deynen. They gave me bread, and I helped them work. It…"

He trailed off, looking back toward the village.

She felt a weight on her chest. She still wished he was more disciplined, but wasn't he, in a way? He was terrible at covering his tracks, but he devoured his books, bounding years ahead of her in Deynen while she barely scraped by, keeping her from jobs that would actually feed him. *Of course*, he didn't know how to avoid leaving footprints in the moss. He was a child, not a Masked One. The only reason he had a life at all was because of what she'd done at the temple. After all she'd seen, all the death, all the fighting, you'd think she—

The serosine.

She looked back at Teros, their eyes meeting as she remembered. He seemed to sense it at the same time.

"Wait," he asked, "why were you—"

She looked back toward the village, dropping into a squat to meet his eyes.

"Teros, I *saw* something. Something that could get us home." Her thoughts suddenly jumbled, her words ten steps ahead of her tongue. "It was serosine, I know it was. They're making it *here,* just like in the war. But if we can find it…"

She looked back at the city, wishing she'd run after the cart. But there was still time, she could still get to it, she…

She looked at Teros again. She'd left work without being paid. She had nothing to feed him, and it would be dark soon. Maybe she was a criminal now, but she'd broken her mask to save this boy, and she shouldn't let him starve for her pride. Even as she longed to get him home — to get both of them home — tonight, they were in the mountains, and she would never give him the life he deserved if she starved him.

"I'm sorry," she said, shaking her head. "It's late. I still have to feed you, but I rushed back from the city. I don't have anything."

She could go back to the village, dig up the little money they had. There might also be another potato in the cave, she—

"It's alright," he said. "They gave me bread. But what are you saying? You saw serosine? In the city?"

She closed her eyes, the image of the serosine returning to her immediately.

She could never forget its shine.

"It was on a wagon by the docks, a big one. They must be making it again, like in the war. You remember the sword, don't you?"

She'd told him about Maegin's sword, leaving out the part where she'd killed the man. Teros was already so wracked with guilt, what good would it have done? But what good was protecting him from the truth, either? If she was going to keep him safe, he'd need to know hard things, to know the difference between strength and weakness.

"I remember," Teros said, frowning. "Uncle Elin told me about it too. His mother was from Deyn. But…what does that have to do with us, Eyri? What can we do about it?"

"We find it," she said, feeling the steel of resolve cooling in her chest, "and we destroy it. If we do that, we can go home."

Teros looked toward the waterfall, where the giant forge stood on the banks of Lake Ce'o, its black water still just visible in the evening light.

"I don't think it's that simple," he said quietly.

Poor Teros. Her brilliant, terrified boy. If she truly deserved to call him hers… Still, he was unlike anyone she'd ever met, ever since the first time she'd seen him in the tower. He deserved to go home. It would be dangerous, but she'd protect him from it. *She* would take the risks, *she* would destroy the serosine. She'd get them back to where they belonged. She'd even help his dreams come true.

"Don't worry," she said, squeezing his shoulder. "I'll be careful. But you want to go back, don't you? You keep saying you wish you could change things back in Zenn."

"I..." he started, opening his mouth before he trailed off.

His face fell as if he might cry. After years without crying, she could still only shed a single tear, and that was only on her most desperate nights. She needed to strengthen him, but she longed to keep his softness too.

"Come on," she said, forcing a smile to her face. "It's getting late, and we should practice. I'll make a plan in the morning."

"Okay," he said quietly. "But if we're going to do this, you have to let me help in the village, at least. I can get to know those people, learn what they know about the forge."

She thought of how happy Teros looked with those other children. Maybe he could have a bigger life than she'd had. He was already so good at Deynen, at talking about big ideas. Maybe when they got home, he would be a diplomat someday. But first, she had to get him out of here.

"Okay," she said, nodding. "You said there was a school?"

9

35ᵗʰ of Sund-z'ar, 970, 8ᵗʰ Year of Iron
10ᵗʰ Day of the War - 'The Running'
Fifteen Years Ago

933 rode his horse along the side of the wagon line, keeping his eyes on the horizon. They should have seen the signal fire by now, but nothing about this war was going as it should. From what he could gather — when you could even *get* information — they were losing, the Zennan troops barely holding on, pushing the Deynens back with wind while the zinc knights held the line at a place called Sesarin, deep in the western flats.

But how could they lose to the bloody Deynens? He'd thought they had nothing but yak herders out east. There were rumors of a new kind of magic, but what did that even mean? The Masked Ones had lost a third of their kind already — not to mention how many human soldiers had fallen. So much for the might of Pen'dil Zenn… But perhaps that was just another lie they told themselves. He scratched his beard under his mask. It had started turning grey, and he'd just lost another food to the Passing. Assuming he didn't die out here, how much time did he really have left?

He watched 732 as she rode ahead of him. *Not 732,* he thought, *Curan.* He preferred to use her spirit's given name, just as she called him Viden. Names turned them back into people, and he loved that little girl — even if the mask proclaimed her as his son. He loved her so much, he could almost forget the other girl he'd had taken from him, the screams that still haunted him at night. Even as he felt death creeping toward him, he found himself clinging to his worthless little life — if only to make sure Curan would be alright.

Unfortunately, his age wasn't the only thing he felt keenly these days. He felt helpless too, the war showing all of them how little they really mattered to the crown. They weren't meant to be fighting on the front — he'd spent a lifetime of favors trying to keep them in the city — but defeat had a way of changing things. As *his* father used to say, when the ground opened up, not even the palace could keep from falling in.

A whistle sounded at the front of the column, signaling a stop. He rode up beside Curan, where she was talking to the wagon drivers. It was such a joy to see her come out of her shell. At thirteen, she was finally losing the quiet from when they broke her with the stone. She was coming into her own, becoming curious again, even as it made him worry for her. She was too honest, too straightforward for the snake pit in the tower. Not that he was much better at politics... After all, he'd thought the Zi'yuns all-powerful, and here they were, marching east, lost in a barren wasteland.

"Come, my son," he said, calling her over. "The horses need to drink."

"I was asking about the water," she said, "but they don't know why it's clear."

Viden looked at the wagon beside them, shaking his head. It *was* strange. Some called the Iron King a fool — rumblings that weren't any fewer with their losses on the battlefield — but the wagons... How could a man who tamed the river be anything but of the gods?

Each wagon was gigantic, some twelve feet long and six feet wide. The thick wood had been brought in from Pen'dil Sohn, but it was still little more than a frame to hold the vessels themselves, clear glass nearly a foot thick full of water from the sacred river. But Curan was right. Why was it clear? When it left the caves, the water was black. He supposed he hadn't thought about it, too baffled by the wagons' mere existence to question further.

He summoned Identity, pulling down a metal trough attached to the wagon's roof. It was on hinges, made so the horses could water easily. He opened the tap, using a combination of Flow and Permanence to turn the spigot. Clever that, using the Principles to lock the water. He'd been told the wagon drivers knew how to open them in an emergency, but it required a special key — and at least three of them to do it.

The horses started drinking greedily, clearly tired from their march. How far had they ridden? The sun was well past halfway through the sky, but with no landmarks in the barrens, it was impossible to tell how much progress they'd made. The wagon driver joined them, freeing his horses from their harness so they could drink as well.

"Sacred One," Kin'ter said, bowing. The man eyed his horses, clearly still nervous to have them drinking from the sacred wagon, but why shouldn't they? After all, the Sacred Mother had created horses just as she'd made Masked Ones, and they all deserved to drink.

"Kin'ter," Viden replied, nodding.

The man stood a few feet away, never coming closer. Still, he was in the army — all the drivers were — so surely he'd be used to Masked Ones, no? At least he talked to Curan easily enough. There was something disarming about a child in a mask, as if the gods wanted to remind them they'd been human once. Finally, Kin'ter cleared his throat, though he only glanced in their direction, afraid to meet his eyes.

"My lord, do you reckon — I mean — do you think we're close? I thought they said we'd see the signal by fourth meal. Not that we have the bells all the way out here, but..."

The man trailed off, shuffling his feet like a child, like he thought a blow was coming. There was far too much fear of Masked Ones. Of course, he didn't blame Kin'ter for that. Unfortunately, he knew all too well how many in the mask deserved to be feared — desired it, even.

"I know," Viden said, scanning the horizon again. "It's strange."

They'd been pushed through a lithium portal with only vague reassurances of what would be waiting for them on the other side. They had more than a hundred Masked Ones — an army in its own right — but it was hard to shake his growing dread. They'd brought every reserve wagon left in the city, but nothing about this assault was adding up. Why send the portal only halfway to the battlefield? Were their supply lines really so splintered they had to reserve lithium? Where was the Iron King's famous strategy? He'd been bold enough to march his army across the stones, and now they were forced to run around like bats in the daylight?

When the horses were finished drinking, Curan lifted the trough back up without needing to be asked. Good girl. He only hoped she didn't do it to preserve his strength. She always seemed worried about him, as if she could save him from the Passing — as if there were any way out of this life other than death. And yet, something in him hoped he could spare her in return... He suddenly felt heavy, like a man made of stone. He'd taught this girl to fight, had taught her to wield her magic, and now he was marching her off to war. What had he really done for her in the end? She still wore the mask, nothing more than a pig he'd prepped for slaughter.

He spotted his captain, 822, coming down the line. He was an ornery man, a chip on his shoulder no doubt earned from having a common crypt number. Still, it was hardly as bad as his own, 933, the sodding third round from the 9-3 vault. Still, even if the captain hated him for it, he flagged the man down. If they were going to force him to take Curan into battle, then he was going to get some bloody answers.

"Yes?" the captain asked, his hand on his sword.

"Where's the portal?" Viden asked. "We should have seen it miles back."

"Use your eyes," the captain replied drily, pointing at the horizon.

Viden looked, suddenly seeing six pillars of smoke against the blue sky. Massive fires burned against the stone, signaling the relay point they'd been marching toward. Oddly, he felt relief. After all, he didn't want Curan starving in the stone barrens. Still, the feeling didn't last. On the other side of the portal was battle — and the impossible task of keeping his girl out of it.

THE END OF PART ONE

A Respite

Pen'dil Deyn - Time Unknown

—:—

So'rek climbed the mountain path, the wind whipping against his back. He tried to pull his robes closer around his shoulders, but there was simply no more fabric. He'd gotten fatter over the winter, and with the ghastly priestly tradition of sewing your own robes, there was nothing for it. His fingers were starting to lock up with arthritis, and he was much too proud to ask one of the novitiates to do it. Still, if he could still make the climb, then he was more than enough of a priest. Even if this was his last winter on this path, it was his bloody grove, and he would see to it. Assuming he could still remember the way…

At the next rise, he stopped, looking around. Sen'el'tul was ahead, its bald head resplendent in the morning sun, the sparkle of the city just visible beyond the other peaks. He put his hands into a triangle, closing one eye as he looked through them at the valley. Placing his thumbs at the base of the tower, he still couldn't see the top of the spire. So, he still had to climb further east…

It was a hell of a way to find your grove, but what else was he to do? They weren't allowed to make maps, and this was how his *nevi'far* had done it. Besides, his wasn't even the strangest way he'd heard of, *thank you very much.* He'd met one priest — an odd bloke who'd saved enough coin to switch guilds — who used to hide pinecones along the mountain paths, grouping them in odd formations that told him which way to go. Seemed like a good way to end up with a lot of pinecones and no idea where your grove was. Fortunately, as his *nevi'far* had always said, the Snow Father chose men for their hearts, not their minds…

He walked another hour or two before turning back to face the city, the tower's spire finally fitting perfectly in the space between his hands. Looking around at the mass of identical crags, he finally spotted his grove. A lightning-shaped crack in the rock only just large enough for a man to pass through, it descended into the darkness. How had his predecessor found this place? It looked like a hundred other chasms in these mountains, and there was no way of knowing from the outside if it would hold a cavern or a cliff.

He stooped down, unlacing his boots as he shook them off, stepping onto the cold stone. His feet were gnarled, the bones bending with age, but there was nothing for it. Perhaps the gods would forgive an old man for stepping on hallowed ground with his shoes on, but after five decades in the priesthood, he refused to abandon his principles now.

He stepped carefully over the rocks, knowing from experience how to find the smooth sections that wouldn't poke him. The moment he reached the crack in the stone, he felt a blast of warmth, his muscles immediately easing despite his long walk through the cold. Sen'el'tul's thermal vents truly were a wonder of the gods. Sometimes, it seemed a pity ordinary Deynens didn't know about these places, though they certainly benefited from their treasures. Unfortunately, secrecy was the only way. If another guild — a profit-seeking guild — knew about these hidden places, it wouldn't be long before they were stripped bare and sold off to Pen'dil Zenn.

So'rek started down the dark tunnel, putting one hand on the stone wall as he felt his way forward. Soon, it felt like being in an oven, the wind of the mountain quickly forgotten as sweat began to bead on his forehead. Again, he thought of the men and women — and if he was honest about the guild's history, it was mostly women — who'd first found these places. The priestesses had been founded by the Snow Father's wife, and they'd nearly crumbled at her death. They'd wandered into the mountains, hoping to die themselves, only to discover the basin's greatest treasure.

Still, he could hardly imagine anyone doing so now. Everyone in Deyn had a purpose now, a sacred mission guiding each step along the path. What would it have taken to stumble through the dark back then, never knowing what the gods would offer you on the other side? If anything, it was a good reminder that he was nothing but a middleman. He hadn't built this place, and though there was pride in caring for it, all he could do was pass it on when the time came.

After a hundred feet or so, the tunnel began to brighten, and finally, he saw a yellow glow on the other end. He emerged into a sort of basin in the stone, open to the air and full of rich volcanic soil. It was hidden well within the crags of the mountain, only truly reachable through his tunnel despite the skylight high above. And there, glowing in the patch of sun, was his grove, nearly two dozen trees bearing hundreds of oranges.

So'rek stood for a long time, hands on hips as he smiled at his fruit. The ache in his bones told him he needed to enjoy this moment. Each time up the mountain could always be your last, of course, but at his age, it was no longer an abstraction. Soon, he'd breathe his last, and the other priests would open his desk, passing on his written instructions to a novice. Soon, all of this would be someone else's to care for. Still, he deserved to say goodbye. After a lifetime in this grotto, it was a part of him.

"Alright, girls," he said, starting down the first row. He chose at random, letting the trees tell him which oranges were ripe. He pulled them off easily — decades of practice barely even shaking the branches as he passed — before dropping them over his shoulder and into the basket on his back.

He barely made it through half the grove before he had to stop, the ache in his muscles telling him he had enough. He'd love to fill his basket, of course, like he had in his youth, but there was only so much a man his age could carry down the slopes. Thankfully for Deyn, even a half-filled basket was an abundance. Without the priests, there'd be no citrus for the common man. They'd all be stuck buying lemons from Zenn, the 'magic' crops going for as much as a townhome in the city center. No, in Deyn, their fruit was for the people. The priests sold some for alms, of course, but mostly it went where it was needed, feeding actual families, keeping them healthy enough to do whatever work the gods had called them to.

He finally stopped, setting down his basket for a moment as he looked through the skylight, his eyes settling on Sen'el'tul.

"Until next time, old friend," he said, bowing his head. He felt a special kinship for El'tul after all these years, but who in Deyn didn't? Every man was a mountain in his own way, each person placed by the gods on a different slope, in a different cave. All they could do was look out at the horizon and abide by the work they'd been given. His had been a simple life, caring for these oranges, but it was a good life, too — an honest life. He looked around the grove one last time, pulling one final orange free and stowing it in his pocket to eat on his way back down.

He might never make it back here, but he'd *grown* something, just as that something had grown inside of him.

———

Pen'dil Yane - Time Unknown

—:—

Aitesi worked the braids into her hair, taking special care with Mamin's old threads to ensure the blue, purple, and green spun perfectly down the sides. As she reached the blue one, she even closed her eyes, pretending it was Mamin's hands on her scalp, imagining she wasn't so alone. More importantly, it helped her ignore the cuts on her fingers, the familiar pain of anyone who worked long hours in the spider silk mills.

Some said the spider weavers had no time for dreams, but this was no ordinary day. The bards were finally letting her take the apprentice exam, and if she passed, she'd never have to touch another spider as long as she lived. Maybe her braids had nothing to do with that, but she felt better pretending Mamin was close, watching over her shoulder. Not to mention the gods... If the whole point of being a Yanewoman was to remember, then there was no greater glory than remembering your Mamin.

Finishing the final weave, she ran her hand over her head one last time, making sure everything was in place. It was hard to tell if they were right without seeing them, but if she passed her exam, she'd never have to guess at her hair again. The apprentices lived in the tower just beyond the pillars, and they probably had mirrors and combs — and fingers that didn't ache from sunup to sundown.

She grabbed her shawl, dashing out the door before the weave woman could rescind her day off — not that the loathsome woman would have an easy time disobeying a Writ of Examination. She also wanted to stop by the pillar one last time before her exam. Even if it was just a good luck charm, something about their whispers made it easier to remember. And lately, the whispers had seemed *urgent,* growing louder in her mind as if they wanted to tell her something. Perhaps they simply wanted her to succeed — after all, it was only after hearing the whispers three months ago that she'd gotten good enough to book her exam.

As she made her way through the winding hills of Yane, she resisted the urge to run. Running in the dark would only attract the city guard, and besides, she didn't want to knock her braids loose. Still, she kept one eye on the sliver of dawn light, refusing to be even a moment late for her exam. The moment the sun touched the top of Sen'el'tul, she'd hurry toward the tower. She just wanted every moment she could get with the pillars first.

As she reached the central square, she saw Ritan, the fish seller who greeted her every morning.

"Aitesi!" he called, raising a withered hand. "Still the only Yanewoman I know who wakes up like a fish."

"And you're the only fisherman I know who doesn't look like one."

He laughed, breathing on his palm and touching it to his forehead.

"Today's the big day?"

"Only the biggest."

"Just so far, girl," Ritan said with a wink. "When you pass—"

"*If* I pass," she said, interrupting.

"*When* you pass," he said again more firmly, "you'll have more big days than you know what to do with."

Aitesi chuckled, shaking her head. They'd had this conversation a hundred times. If only she could recite her arguments with Ritan for her exam. Still, he'd already proven himself kinder than anyone she'd met since Mamin died, and he'd fed her more times than she'd like to admit, the meager meals at the spider weavers making her stomach seize with hunger.

"Fine," she said. "When I pass, I'll use my bard's salary to shower you in fish."

"I've got fish, girl," Ritan said, gesturing at this cart, though it didn't seem as full these days, his arthritis no doubt making it hard to handle the nets. "All I want is to brag about you to the other old farts. 'I know Aitesi,' I'll say, 'the greatest bard who ever lived.'"

"Just wait 'til I write a song about you."

She breathed on her own palm, bowing to him before she made her excuses, eager to reach the pillar before the test.

Even in the early morning light, the pillars were perfect, glittering like jewels in the central square. There was a woman already praying at them, her forehead on the ground, so Aitesi walked around to the other side, resting her own head against the metal between her palms. It was cool against her forehead, the nights still brisk even for the spring. Immediately, the whispers came to her, calming her as they forced the worry from her mind.

She began reciting the Ode to the Distant Star, letting the tempo of the whispers guide her. Some said it was bad luck to practice on the day of your exam, but those were pompous rich boys with more money than sense. It didn't matter to them if they passed or failed; they could always go work for their fathers in the nice shops on the King's Bluffs. Almost no one escaped the spider silk weavers, and she wasn't going to add to that number for lack of practice. She—

Sitosarunal, the pillar whispered.

Aitesi gasped, pulling her head from the pillar as a brilliant glow filled her eyes. Or was it in her mind? She whipped around, finding the sun just cresting Sen'el'tul, bathing the pillar in its light. A trick of the eye, maybe? But she could have sworn she'd heard the pillar say something. It always whispered, of course, but they were little fragments of speech, nothing a person would ever recognize. Or, at least, not in any language she'd ever heard… Still, this was something new. She—

"Aitesi!" Ritan called, waving from across the square. "It's time!"

He was right, of course. The sun waited for no one, least of all a weaver from the west cliffs. Aitesi took a deep breath, trying to summon the stillness she'd felt just moments ago. There would be plenty of time to explore the mysteries of the basin as a bard. Before that, she needed to become one.

PART TWO

A Journal

Cesium is the answer. It's not a mineral I'd ever heard of before, but the Snow Father mentions it in his journal more than once. He seemed to think it made the water black, but isn't that the color of all water? Still, the concentrations I need to perfect the cobalt are higher than what I can get from the river. Is there a way to collect it?

-Journal of Serimh nal Akistore:
960th Year of Finding, 12th of Ciromira

—:—

10

Eyri saw her brother's face. It was dark, and she'd been wandering in a strange place. There were logs all around her, but they were planted in the ground, their tops covered in leaves. Were they trees? She'd never been to Sohn, but they were so odd, unlike any plant she'd seen in Zenn. Wait…she—

Borash. She spun in a circle looking for him. How had she forgotten? She could have sworn she'd seen his outline in the darkness, his voice whispering her name. But the trees wouldn't stop rustling in the wind. The place was full of voices, thousands of them calling to her.

Kouselumakash, a voice whispered behind her.

She spun again, her hand reaching for her sword, but it was gone. She wore nothing but a frock, like the one she'd had as a little girl, with flowers Mems had stitched onto the shoulders. Still, as she turned, she suddenly noticed a break in the trees ahead, the moon filling it from above.

She wandered into the clearing, the voices of the trees suddenly falling silent. There was tall grass growing there, like the kind they filled baskets with from Seln. Only it wasn't dry and yellow, its fronds lush and green as they reached for her. She followed a path through the grass, looking over her shoulder. Anything could be hiding between those too-tall plants. What if there was another Masked One hiding there, waiting to strike her down? They would only be doing justice for her crimes, of course, but she looked all the same. It seemed part of her still thought she deserved to live.

As she reached the center of the clearing, the grass fell away, leaving her standing on stone again. In fact, she couldn't even see the trees any longer, the smooth dark rock stretching out in all directions. She could hear the sound of water from somewhere, but it wasn't constant like the river. It came in and out, like the snoring of a giant. Still, she couldn't see its source. All she could make out in the moonlight was a giant pile of rubble.

She walked toward the nearest piece. It looked like a giant hunk of metal, broken into shards like a clay pot. It was the size of her chest, and it leaned haphazardly against a dozen others. It had one smooth edge, as if it had been a giant block before some god decided to smash it. Even in the moonlight, it seemed to glow with its own light. It seemed to call to her, and she reached for it, the whispers surging back into her mind.

Eyri—

She lurched up from bed, breathing heavy. Who had called her name? She looked around the cave, but Teros was asleep next to her, curled up as he always was, one arm still draped across her. Luckily, she hadn't woken him. She gently took his hand, putting it by his side. He rolled over, muttering in his sleep, though he quickly quieted down again. His nightmares were worse than hers, and she hated how helpless she felt on the nights she had to rock him back to sleep, his tears wetting her robes.

As she sat there, watching Teros, she felt the wind against her face. It was rare to feel it blow into their cave, though the air sometimes swirled oddly in the mountains. Everything here was—

She froze, a strand of Identity curling around her in the air. She hadn't seen the Principles in months, but she'd know it anywhere, a lifetime of magic making it like another appendage — albeit one she'd lost. She reached for it in her mind, but it disappeared. Was she seeing things? A remnant from her dream maybe?

She got up, tiptoeing out of the cave. There were a few embers left of their fire, and she sat by it. The nights were still cold in the mountains, much colder than it would have been back home for spring. She looked up through the crack in the rock, taking in the stars. Would she find what she was looking for out here?

She'd begun looking for the serosine, taking jobs closer to the Zinc Quarter. Unfortunately, the jobs she'd found weren't much better than the ones she'd had in the city center, wasting her days with toil without much to show in the way of reconnaissance. Still, she was slowly working on a map of the area south of the waterfall, hoping to learn how to get closer to the forge.

She needed a job *inside* the quarter if she was really going to find the serosine. She'd need to track their shipments and find a way inside to burn the metal. But shouldn't she do more? What if she destroyed the forge itself? It had felt wrong leaving it intact after the war, but the generals hadn't wanted the Deynens to revolt. In a way, it was the *true* god here, more powerful than some silly poems about the Snow Father. It would probably be impossible to do alone, but if it meant saving her people…

She sighed, taking a piece of moss and tossing it into the embers. It slowly crackled as it heated, smoke rising from its surface before it became a flame. She could have used more sleep, but once her mind started spinning, she knew better than to roll around in her bed for nothing. Even if she never found any answers through her constant stewing… She was just as helpless as she'd been the entire time in Deyn.

She looked back at the cave, just barely able to make out the shape of Teros sleeping. At least she felt like more of a mother now. He'd started at the school, the village leaders having her sign some sort of guild document in Deynen. Teros said they would garnish his wages when he was of age since she wasn't a guild member, but otherwise it was free. All she'd have to give them was one free day of labor each month, usually before the holidays. It was a good deal. Hopefully, she'd have him back home before he got old enough to worry about repaying them. And in the meantime, they would feed him a meal each morning, keeping him from starving while she figured out the serosine.

Still, he seemed happier now, *lighter* somehow. Each day when she picked him up, he babbled to her the whole way back, telling her everything he'd learned. Now, he even did his sword practice without complaint, letting her go so far as to teach him to throw her knife. He'd mostly missed the wide clump of moss she'd set up against the rocks, but he hadn't given up, throwing it again and again until the blade went in. He'd actually *cheered* when he hit it, the first time she'd ever seen him excited about something outside of a book.

She wiped a hand over her face, chuckling to herself. He was such a wonder. She had no real claim to him — and certainly no share of the credit for how brilliant he was — but he felt like her boy all the same. Could she become a mother worthy of him? Without the mask, she was just a poor girl from Mer'n Hill. She wasn't royalty like he was, and she'd made them both criminals at the temple. Still, she had to believe. If she could find the serosine and remove the stain from their names, maybe they could be free. Maybe they could have a life again.

She watched the moss as it crackled in the fire. She pretended she was back in Zenn, imagining the fire was in an actual grate. She imagined the walls around her, the tiny house she bought for her and Teros. She closed her eyes, letting it be real for just a moment. She had to find the serosine, had to make it all come true.

11

12ᵗʰ of Selomira 979
Rule of the Vindeista
(14ᵗʰ of Perat-kam, 985, 23ʳᵈ Year of Iron)

After a long night by the fire, Eyri finally found herself back in the city, taking the long, arcing road around Lake Ce'o to the Zinc Quarter. The sun was over Sen'el'tul, the light glittering off the black water as it flowed back into the caverns from the waterfall. As many times as she'd trudged up the hill in the past few months, it felt strange to come *this* way around the lake in the morning.

The road was already busy despite the early hour, but not everyone was in a hurry. Every so often, she would pass someone sitting by the banks, eating their morning meal or praying in the strange way of the Deynens, their tiny zinc knives pressed against their foreheads. It *was* beautiful in its own way, so much sacred water in one place — and outside the caves — but she could never seem to see it as they did. She remembered this place as an inferno, a mountain of serosine melting as the fire burned against her skin, only the porcelain of her mask protecting her face.

They'd pushed it all into the water, everything they'd destroyed hidden in its black depths save for the pieces of the dam still sticking up in places. Maybe the Deynens prayed here for solace, but to her, this place would always be more of a tomb than a temple. Even worse, what right did these people have to seek the gods when they were pouring death back into the basin? Did they know their precious lords were making serosine again? Had they learned nothing from defeat?

The Quarter itself was unrecognizable, surrounded now by thick stone walls, the windows of the buildings with metal shutters on the sides. They'd made this place a castle, clearly spending the last two decades preparing to fight again. Only this time, it seemed they'd hold the Quarter even if the city fell, leaving the rest of the Deynens to their fate.

Eyri felt her teeth clench, her nails digging into her palms as the old tightness dug into her shoulder. As she entered the Quarter, she felt lucky she hadn't brought her sword — not that the knights standing guard at the gates would have let a Zennan woman in if she was armed. Still, it took everything in her not to draw her dagger from its hiding place in her robes. But what good would it do to slit the throat of a single knight when they were forging swords by the hundreds? Even in a child's hands, a pound of serosine could bring a dozen Masked Ones to their knees.

The guards gave her a cursory glance, but the Quarter wasn't technically closed to the public. Some of the merchants she'd worked for had sent their assistants over for one thing or another, though the difference from the rest of the city remained clear. This was a military place, run by killers, not merchants. There was no food in sight, nothing for sale except metal. Smithies lined the streets, and knights walked in all directions, their plate seeming to clank in time with the pounding of the anvils.

She'd stayed on the fringes the past two days, taking up whatever odd jobs she could. Still, metal was heavy, and the work was difficult. The blacksmiths seemed to have more apprentices than other merchants in the city, and she'd mostly been stuck hauling ingots or coal with little to show in the way of reconnaissance. Yesterday, one man had actually paid her a few siulkiys, but even after months of being paid in potatoes, some coins felt like a pittance compared to what she was really looking for. That morning, she turned toward the waterfall, desperate to get closer to the forge.

The city center loomed overhead above the waterfall, but the forge was somehow more imposing. Nestled into the cliffs and made of black stone, she could have mistaken it for a fortress had it not been for the massive column of smoke pouring from its chimney. Ringed with a fence of shining steel, it had its own grounds teeming with workers. She couldn't see the forge itself in the dim of the cavernous building, but during the war they'd said its bellows never went quiet. Perhaps to a Deynen, this was a good place, a normal place. But knowing what they were making, the buzzing of the workers seemed insidious, each one rushing to cast more death out into the valley.

There was a cobblestone square in front of the forge with a statue of the old zinc lord — the one she'd watched them behead after the war — and she stood in its shadow watching the gates. She tried to look casual, standing with her arms folded, though her eyes darted back and forth. Why hadn't they killed more of the Deynen leadership? The new zinc king had supposedly fought his way up through the ranks after the Zennan army left, but with this serosine, it seemed he — and all his generals — were just as bad as the others.

Wagons were already coming and going, with what looked like raw materials coming through the east and finished goods through the west. There was a wagon already leaving, laden with metal, but it looked like zinc instead of serosine — and it wasn't covered with a cloth either, the Deynens clearly knowing which products they needed to hide. Workers came in through the front, though they scattered in all directions once they reached the grounds. She began to count the guards, though there was an incredible number, at least a dozen stationed and another dozen on patrol.

"Udvi im haen," a stern voice said from behind her.

She knew the word for *hands* from the docks, at least, and she turned slowly, her palms turned up. There was a zinc knight behind her, his hand on his sword. His helmet had a strip of gold along the brow, marking him a captain.

"For foreigner, this not place, little woman."

He seemed to recognize her for a Zennan, hissing at her in a heavy accent, though his words were backwards like they always were in Deyn.

She met his eyes, her rage threatening to boil over. Little woman? She wasn't afraid of all that plate like every other fool in the basin. Even without her sword, she could have her knife under his helmet before he could blink. She'd killed Masked Ones, and he thought she'd be scared of some rust-blower from the war? *Little woman.* But…of course, that's all she was now — all she'd ever be unless she found that serosine. If she could really kill them all she would, but this was a different task. She had to live long enough to uncover the truth, to be Zenn's eyes and not its blade.

"Sculdyi," she said, apologizing as she bowed. He kept his eyes on her as she walked away, scurrying toward the shade of a row of smithies on the other side of the square. She turned the next corner where she finally stopped, leaning against a wall. She tilted her head back, closing her eyes as she sighed.

How was she supposed to take down a forge she couldn't even look at? Even worse, how was she meant to do it alone? She'd gotten used to doing her own work over the years, but she'd had magic then, the power of the gods to wield. But even as a Masked One, would she have been able to accomplish anything without the king's authority? She was a blade, true, but there was no one to wield her now. She was—

"Are you looking for some metal?" a voice asked.

She turned, finding a tiny old man looking at her as he leaned out a window of the building she'd leaned against. He had a bald head and bushy white eyebrows.

"You speak Zennan?" she asked.

"That I do. My peppin had more dreams than smarts, thought I might make something of myself if I learned. That was before the war, of course…"

"You must be talented, working so close to the forge."

He laughed.

"Maybe, or stubborn. I'm the only smithy who speaks Zennan, though, that's for sure. That's not why you came?"

She shook her head.

"I'm looking for work, actually. I…know a bit about forging if you could use the help. Or I could carry things."

He looked her up and down.

"Come around the other side," he said, pointing around the corner.

She came around what was apparently the front of the building where there was an entryway wide enough for a cart, its door split down the middle with one side propped open. The old man had sat on a small anvil by the window, and he pointed her toward a chair in the center of the room. It was actual wood from Sohn, polished to a shine.

"So, you know some forging. How much is some?"

"I can fix chips, sharpen blades, things like that."

"And where'd you learn a thing like that?" he asked.

"My paps," she lied. "He was a smith in the war, kept it up a bit when he got home."

"Nice blades in Zenn," he said. "Even if Deyn made all the really deadly ones."

He looked back at the rest of the shop and she followed his eyes. There was a large iron forge in the back and a workbench with two more anvils in the center of the room. The far wall had a half-dozen swords hanging on it, some of them clearly made for knights.

"I guess I could use some help. I don't do a lot of orders, but the ones I get take time, and my grandson's too busy to help these days. Could probably only pay you a thi'riy a month, but if you want it, it's yours."

A thi'riy? That was a hundred times what she'd made at any of her other jobs. More importantly, she'd have somewhere to go in the Quarter each day, getting her just a block away from the forge. She stood, giving him a bow. Even if he was from Deyn, he surely knew enough of Zenn to understand the gratitude of a half bow.

"I'd be honored," she said.

"Alright," he said, chuckling as he waved a hand. "But there's no need for all that. What's your name?"

"Eyri," she said.

"A good name," he said, nodding. "I'm Chir Chiremir. I got a shipment of new iron coming in tomorrow. Be here early to unload it and we'll see what you can do."

12

Elin nir Dek'rc rode at the bow of the ship, hands behind his back as he stared into the darkness. Even though he could hardly see the cave around him, he could still tell they were moving quickly, cutting through the water like a giant fish. It was a wonder they could move so at this speed upstream, but he supposed that was the point of using a boat from Pen'dil Sing. With all their iron, Sing had always had more children than they knew what to do with, the boat choking with sailors. At least that meant plenty of hands for rowing…

Suddenly, flames appeared in the darkness, filling two massive glass tubes affixed to the cavern wall. They lit a fork in the river to their left, and the boat lurched to take the turn. Elin looked behind him, the Light Bringer refusing to meet his eyes from where he stood next to the captain. He seemed offended a Zennan had been allowed to witness the famous secrets of Sing's "Imperial Navy," but how could you deny a guest of the emperor himself?

Besides, it wasn't as if Elin would remember the route. They'd turned dozens of times, always suddenly, and the flames disappeared as quickly as they were lit, plunging the cavern back into darkness. He also didn't have a clue how the magic worked. He could see Passion rising from the Light Bringer's hands, but he couldn't tell how he knew those bulbs would be there, trapping the oxygen in the cave for him to burn.

Thankfully, he didn't need their parlor tricks. The Light Bringer — and those like him — could never seem to understand that the Duke of Remembrance didn't need their petty magic. Even the path to Sing was nothing to him. He had lithium, and when he finally returned to Sing to be crowned, he'd appear out of the air like a flame himself, the cowards rushing to bow before him. In fact, his first decree would be to put this Light Bringer to death, so everyone could watch as his robes turned into one final glorious flame.

"We're almost there, sir," a steward said at his side.

"Ah, thank you," Elin said, nodding. He'd been caught unawares, something about the darkness dragging him into this constant dreaming. He needed to remember he didn't do this for his own glory. He would conquer, yes, but he would do it to save the valley. Even if his success humbled his lessers, he must refuse to relish in it.

"Could you get my aide? He'll want to join me."

"Yes, my lord," the steward said with a bow.

The crew seemed to move all at once, bursting into a flurry of activity as they prepared to dock. Half the men continued rowing, of course, but the other half began to go below deck, no doubt in a rush to unload their cargo and start another run. If a Sing ship wasn't on the river every minute, was the river really running?

151 appeared in the scrum, moving slowly through the crowd as it parted around him. Most of the sailors looked like they'd never seen a Masked One before, and one sailor even looked away, touching his thumb to his heart in prayer. If only they knew. 151 was just a pet, a toy. The real magic lay in the maskless duke hiding in plain sight. At least by the time he was finished, the world would know what true power was.

"Lord Dek'rc," 151 said, nodding as he joined him.

"Everything good below deck?"

"As good as can be expected. No one looked in the crates — not with me standing there, at least. Can't say it didn't make them curious, though."

Sunlight appeared ahead, forcing him to blink as his eyes adjusted. The gap in the caverns was brief in Sing, but he could see a crack of sky, and it looked like a precious jewel after so many days in the dark. They burst into the light, suddenly surrounded by other boats as they entered the port. They didn't stop in the main port, though. They sailed on, passing under the legs of the giant iron statue of Föhr nol Serint. The old man looked like a flame himself, his rusting beard catching the sun as it wound down around his chest. There was little that impressed him — even with all the pleasures Sing had to offer — but the statue somehow always managed to, like another Sen'el'seng. He couldn't wait to rule over it.

Before long, they reached the gilded docks of the palace, the next stretch of cavern rising up ahead. The boat pulled in, though the sailors hurried out of the way as soon as they were tied off. Palace attendants began to storm the decks, taking up the serosine from the hold. It was stored in actual wooden crates from Sohn, but at least the metal was valuable enough to merit the expense. Too bad he'd be destroying this batch when he took the city someday.

Elin turned away, staring at the palace while the work went on behind him. Shaped like a giant flower, the palace dome held hundreds of petals made of stone, encircling the golden statue of the Wise Father at the top. Most incredible of all were the windows. Each one no bigger than your palm, they were made of hundreds of different colors, the famed glass blowers of Sing no doubt spending a lifetime to get them right.

Finally, he saw a Light Bringer emerge from the palace doors, her own army of attendants marching behind her. She was dressed in full regalia, her robes visible even from the docks as they danced with greens and pinks. Some said it took a thousand hours to stitch the flowers on their robes, but it was clearly time well spent. Elin looked over his shoulder at the ship's Light Bringer, suppressing a smirk as he watched the man's eyes bulge. This woman would outrank him by at least a dozen steps, and it might be the last time he ever saw one of her kind in his short, miserable career on the ships.

You see, he thought, *your secrets are nothing compared to mine.*

Still, it wasn't time to be smug. His real work was beginning, and he ought to be about it. 151 moved without needing to be asked, pausing the workers on the gangplank so Elin could walk down to meet his host.

"Elin nir Dek'rc," the Light Bringer said, stopping just short of the crates as he approached. "I am the Fohlense; we exchanged letters. It seems you delivered after all?"

"I'm a man of my word," he said.

Her eyes flicked to the right, taking in 151. He hadn't mentioned he'd be bringing a guest. Perhaps she was considering if her Passion could overwhelm the Masked One's if it came to blows. A useful distraction. After all, in a fight, it wasn't the Masked One she should fear. Of course, by the time she learned that lesson, it would be too late. No matter how strong their fire was in Sing, true power was in precision and control. That's why Zennan magic would eventually rule the entire valley. They just needed his steady hands to guide it.

"We'll see about that," she said, "assuming your metal is as powerful as you promised."

He bowed his head. The serosine was real, alright. So real, it would get him next to the emperor.

"The prince would like to see you," she continued. "To thank you personally for this…contribution to our cause. I assume you're amenable?"

"Absolutely."

She met his eyes. There was a heat to them that went beyond the fire pulsing through her veins. She didn't trust him, of course, but she wasn't sure why, and that was the only opening he needed.

"Follow me," the Fohlense said, turning back toward the palace.

Today he'd see a prince, but soon it'd be the emperor. It was slow going, but he didn't mind. He wanted to take his time. He was building a true kingdom, one that would last for generations. He may as well make sure the walls were sturdy on his palace before he took the throne.

13

Eyri's face was wet with sweat, her face stuck in Chir's forge. The old man sat on an anvil behind her, looking over her shoulder as he taught her how to arrange the coals. All the forge work she'd done at the tower had been haphazard at best, the furnaces choking with coal, with the repairs on her sword left to be done in haste between jobs. This was more like…*music*, everything arranged just so, Chir controlling the heat like a band leader.

"Good," he said with a nod, the signal she could shut the forge door.

She stayed squatted by it, looking through the tiny grate as the flames grew.

"You're not afraid of a little flame," Chir said. "That's good."

She almost laughed. It was hotter without a porcelain mask on her face, but she certainly knew her way around a fire.

"I learned young," she said instead.

He motioned for her to join him at the work table. There was a massive sword on it, the blade shining with zinc. It was unlike any zinc sword she'd ever seen, though, a fork running up its center with an amalgam on each tong. One was mercury like her sword, but the other shone bright like silver.

"This is *Vandraeb,* my grandson's sword. The Killer of Winds."

"You made this?" she asked.

"It's my life's work," he said, tilting his head toward the east. The only thing in that direction was the massive stadium where the zinc knights fought each other, another relic they'd left intact after the war — though it was another she was starting to think they shouldn't have. "My grandson's fighting in the duels. He has another bout tomorrow, but we need to fix his sword first."

The sword seemed perfect, but as she looked closer, she saw a tiny chip at the end of one of the forks. Or was it simply blunted, rammed into something hard? It would be hard to use a sword like that. There was no doubt it was meant more for directing the wind rather than meeting other blades. Unfortunately, with swords, you rarely got to draw them without someone else drawing theirs.

"How do you fix something so delicate?" she asked. The damaged part wasn't large, but it crossed into the vein of silver on the upper prong. She'd fixed the steel edge of her blade a hundred times, but she'd never damaged her amalgam.

"You let it fix itself."

Chir took the sword — incredibly still able to lift it in one hand despite his age — and turned toward the forge, sticking it into the glowing coals. With the sword between them, she finally noticed the pattern in how he'd had her lay them, the embers forming a sort of bed for the blade. Before long, the metal had turned red, the amalgams seeming to *pulse* under the heat.

"Now watch," Chir said. "Keep your eye on that blunted tip."

She stared hard at the blade, though it was hard not to blink in the light of the fire. As she watched, the sword began to *move,* the broken prong seeming to unfurl until the blade was whole again. Chir grabbed it by the hilt, quickly dunking it into a giant urn that reached up to the man's chest. It was full of black water like the lake, only thicker, as if the river had been turned to honey. The sword hissed as it went in, and Chir wiped his hands.

"Now we wait."

He went back to his workbench, seemingly unfazed by the magic he'd just performed. She'd felt the horrible gales from zinc swords during the war, had seen how powerful they were, but this… It was only then she truly realized why, during the war, they'd ripped the zinc blades from their hilts after each battle.

"How…" was all she managed to say as Chir waved for her to join him.

"It's something of the gods," he said. "A combination of Arikai nol D'ek, the Snow Father, and the first Zinc Lord. But in Deyn, swords have souls; they remember. If you treat them like kin, they'll repay you with their memories."

She was about to ask him more when there was a sound at the door. There was a tall young man standing outside, speaking to someone she couldn't see across the street. She supposed he might be considered handsome, but she'd spent too long behind the mask to know what that really meant anymore. Did she fancy men like him? Did she fancy men at all? Raising Teros had come naturally, but every other aspect of "womanhood" made her feel like a stranger to herself.

"Well," Chir said, "speaking of kin, that's the owner of *Vandraeb* himself."

The young man waved goodbye to whoever he was talking to outside, finally ducking through the doorway. He was tall, built like a knight, though he wore a dress uniform instead of plate. She tried to remember the Deynen ranks, but he must have been of the Third Zamak, three triangles stitched into his sleeve.

"Sonote, this is my new assistant, Eyri. She's from Zenn, but she knows her way around a forge."

"Nice to meet you," Sonote said with a nod, surprisingly speaking Zennan himself, though he had more of an accent than his grandfather. "Is my sword ready?"

"Very nearly," Chir said. "Why don't you test it?"

Sonote walked up to the vat, peering down into the dark liquid.

"Sonote has an important duel tomorrow," Chir explained. "How was your training today?"

"Alright," the boy said, though he didn't take his eyes from the blade. He glanced at his grandfather, his eyes narrowed.

"They say the zinc lords are nervous, that they might use *piabbelt* rules against me. I'll never find a second, the way we've pushed through the ranks and—"

For a moment, Chir's face fell, the first time she'd seen him without a smile, but he still raised a hand, stopping his grandson.

"Don't worry. It's all for the best. It just means we're getting to them. If they come at you with two, then you'll just have one more to kill."

Sonote's mouth formed a thin line. She'd always thought the Deynens relished their duels, but this felt like something else entirely. The boy muttered to himself in Deynen, turning back to the sword.

"Draebucc im svakro megre lof."

He took the sword by its hilt, pulling it from the liquid. Despite its thickness, it ran off the blade like water. The amalgams shone in the light from the door, the sword gleaming, completely fixed. *Healed* felt like a bridge too far, but it didn't change the miracle of what she'd seen. Sonote flexed his arm, slowly swinging the blade. Suddenly, a breeze rushed through the smithy, rippling against her robes. Had the sword caused it, or was it luck?

Chir stood, squeezing his grandson's shoulder.

"Bodh fin im gepin mishlo. Topacre."

She didn't understand a word, but Sonote slowly nodded, meeting his grandfather's eyes.

"Topacre," Chir repeated.

They both looked at her as if they'd forgotten she was there.

"Now," Chir said, turning to Sonote as he rubbed his forehead, "we need more forge water. Your mother wants you home for dinner, but will you take Eyri to the quartermaster first? They'll need to know her if she'll be assisting me."

Eyri followed Sonote out into the street, the young man staying a step ahead of her with his long legs. She felt like his squire or something, scurrying behind him in her white robes. Still, her heart pounded with excitement. Her first day in this job and she was already getting to go to the forge? If Chir let her do trips on her own, she'd be hunting for the serosine in no time...

"Why did you come to Deyn?" Sonote asked, glancing over his shoulder. She almost hadn't heard him, lost in thought as she was, but her lie was well-rehearsed.

"I came for my son. His father was from Deyn, but he passed, and now I need to work."

Sonote grunted. He didn't seem like one who trusted easily — although that made his grandfather all the rarer. It was helpful that Chir spoke Zennan, of course, but why trust her to work in his smithy? They were an odd family, to be certain, especially if they were foolhardy enough to challenge the knights in their duels.

"Are you…excited for your next duel?" she asked Sonote's back.

"No," he said, not bothering to turn.

With that, they reached the forge gates. She looked over her shoulder, afraid the knight from the other day would spot her, but Sonote took her right up to the guards.

"Nes sva'haen im mem gep. Teshtara smef'alo bodh fin."

The guard looked her up and down, nodding. Apparently satisfied, he scribbled something on a piece of parchment, waving them through. Chir led her under the gate, taking her around the side of the building.

"Next time you come, tell them you are *'sva'haen im Chir nir Chiremir'* and they'll let you in. Go nowhere but the quartermaster and you'll keep your hands."

She most certainly wouldn't confine herself to the quartermaster, but by then, she'd be ready to kill whoever barred her path, "little woman" or not.

On the right side of the building, carved into the dark stone, was what must have been the quartermaster. A dozen men crowded around a window in the stone, shouting for supplies. It was a wonder they got anything done, but when Sonote appeared, the crowd parted around his uniform. He seemed to take it all in stride, marching to the front as he ordered the forge water.

A quartermaster's assistant ran to the front with a large jar the size of her chest, placing it in front of Sonote with a bow. Sonote nodded to it, and Eyri picked it up, the liquid surprisingly light. He turned, leading her back to the gate.

"I'll let you find your way back," he said, nodding as he turned to go.

"Thank you," she called after him, but he didn't turn around, disappearing into the crowd. Still, she couldn't blame him. She'd dueled herself for a time, and while the Masked Ones didn't *try* to kill each other, she knew the weight fighting could put on your shoulders.

She hurried back to Chir's, her mind spinning as she thought through a hundred different ways to reach the forge. It *was* a kindness they were doing for her, but she refused to be deterred. Even if she worked for Chir, it was just a step on her path back to her own people. They seemed like good men, but they were none of her concern. She only hoped they'd find a way to survive once she killed their god.

14

Serimh woke to banging on his door. He opened his eyes, hoping he was dreaming, but the fist pounded against the wood again. The blue light of morning had barely reached his room, so it had to be early. Still, for however rough the banging was, it was a wonder they'd chosen to give him a door at all. The knights had made it clear on multiple occasions they thought nothing of his privacy — in fact, they frequently showed him the keys to his rooms. So, why give him the dignity of dressing himself now?

Unwilling to find out the hard way, he forced himself from his tiny bed. His bad hip was stiff — another unfortunate sign he was aging in captivity — but he managed to reach the door before the banging resumed again. He wrenched it open, finding three knights outside. He recognized the one in the middle, the one who'd been watching him in the forge.

"Priest," the knight said, his old title clearly meant to demean him, "the Zinc Lords want to see you."

"See me? I thought they were happy with you dogs to do their bidding."

The knight chuckled, though he looked like he would love nothing more than to snap Serimh's neck, his eyes dark under his helmet.

"Even brought by a dog, it's a summons all the same. Perhaps you'd like to dress yourself properly."

Serimh looked down at his night robes. They were a sumptuous kelo wool, one of the few luxuries he'd managed to procure in this godsforsaken place. He felt his neck grow hot.

"Certainly," he said, slamming the door.

He looked around his room, suddenly unable to recognize it. What could this mean? He'd finished the serosine, the knights carting it off to the gods knew where. Unfortunately, in the few days he'd had off — between all his other tedious responsibilities at the forge — he'd made little progress on his predicament. He'd sent a few letters — in code, of course, since the knights clearly read his mail — but he hadn't heard anything yet, none of his old friends willing to vouch for him apparently. He'd have to reach farther, dig deeper into his contacts. Of course, that would mean more risk, more—

But wait, what could this summons be? Did they know about his plans? Had someone ratted him out? He hurried toward his dresser, yanking it open as he sifted through his clothes. He could hear the knights laughing in the hallway. Whatever this was, he'd better be quick about it. It seemed the variables were always changing on him. Unfortunately, in Deyn, what you didn't know was almost always the thing that got you killed.

Soon after — his robes barely closed around him — Serimh was being ferried down the hill on horseback. He'd been unceremoniously hoisted into a saddle of his own, and now he was caught between the knights, as if they thought he might try to run. Unfortunately, these men didn't understand him at all. He *did* want to run, yes, but he'd done his duty this long, hadn't he?

He wasn't disloyal to Deyn exactly. He just obeyed the gods first, and they'd brought him into the world for science. Even if he'd realized he couldn't reach the gods with shackles on his hands, it hardly made him a traitor. Of course, the lords wouldn't see it that way… It made his mind spin again. What was this summons about, really?

Below them, the forge was just visible in the predawn light, its smoke floating over the lake. The ride down the hill was always such a pain. Of course, he'd been the one who begged to stay in the city center. He was on the zinc floor of the sacred tower, so they could still watch him easily, but part of him knew it'd be suicide to move down to the Quarter. That way, at least, he was still close to the artifelians — and what was left of his family — which would hopefully give him the tiniest head start when he finally chose to run away. The cousins he'd already written to had been relatively unsympathetic, of course, but he couldn't give up yet. Even if none of his friends would take him in, family couldn't turn you away when you showed up on their doorstep, could they?

The strong Deynen horses, at least, never complained, and as they came down the bottom of the hill, the little tower appeared. Sitting next to the stadium, it was bathed in smoke from the smithies. Like everything else in Deyn, it too had changed since the war, its stone sides gleaming with all manner of spikes, the windows now adorned with metal shutters. The knights had never really worshipped the Snow Father — an original sin, perhaps, of Deyn putting their army under a separate king — but even the Zinc Father was being forgotten in their haste. These men worshipped war, and they spent every day preparing for its return.

But weren't their duels today? You'd think they had better things to do, but perhaps this was the only time all the Zamaks would be gathered together. But what did that have to do with him? What did that—

"We're to take you in the servants' entrance, priest," the lead knight said over his shoulder. "Try not to touch anything; it's all rather sharp."

The other knights chuckled, spurring their horses as they sped ahead, opening the rear gates to the tower. The courtyard was already buzzing with activity, the sound of hooves almost deafening as knights of every kind scurried across the paving stones. Still, no one looked at him as they passed, handing their horses to a battalion of liveried servants as they entered the little tower.

They took the first stairwell to the right, winding toward the Room of Memory. All the torches were lit, but otherwise the place was drab as ever. He'd been a young priest when he was first summoned here all those years ago, but he could still remember how *sumptuous* everything had been then. A thick rug used to run up the stairs, and every wall had been covered with some kind of animal fur from the spring hunts. Apparently, in Iremi nal Miri's fortress there was to be no joy. A new king with new gods indeed.

They reached the Room of Memory, another pair of knights already waiting for them just outside the giant steel doors. They nodded, swinging the doors open to reveal the entire Lords' Council in session. They sat in a circle around their giant brazier, each one's sword standing up before them, stuck into the stone. The king sat directly across from the door, his face shrouded in flame, but the glint of *Eng'ideref* — the true sword — was still visible. For a sword that held the memory of the basin, how strange for it to be wielded by a man who cared so little for the past.

Unfortunately, it seemed only one memory mattered to the king — or to anyone in the basin, for that matter. Behind him on the wall hung six porcelain masks. Taken from the demons in the war, rumor had it the king had killed them all himself. Each mask had been cracked in a hundred places like the strange pottery from Sing, the fissures repaired with molten zinc. They seemed to shine in the dark recesses of the room, their empty eyes always watching. Imagine seeing such a thing on the battlefield... He didn't blame these men their scars, of course, only their...*single-mindedness.* The world was larger than their squabbles — if they'd only care to look.

"Serimh nal Akistore," the king said slowly, his voice like cracking ice. "I trust you appreciate the honor in your being here?"

"My lord," Serimh said, bowing despite the protests from his hip. "This is a holy place. Of course, I am most humbly grateful."

The king chuckled.

"Perhaps you would have made a better politician than a priest. No matter, it seems you were successful with the serosine. More successful than we'd hoped."

Serimh said nothing. It was best not to speak unless asked something directly. Given his rank, he was also meant to keep his eyes on the flames, lest they stray to the sword and its sacred memories.

"We bring you here," the king continued, "to allow you to prove yourself once more. The serosine is only the beginning."

He looked up at that, though he quickly forced his eyes back on the brazier. So he hadn't been caught yet... But what more could they possibly want? The metal he'd already made was enough for three wars, let alone what the Zennans would do to them when they found out.

"At least it seems you recognize the importance of your task," Lord Stal said from the next chair in the circle. "Do we presume correctly that your priestly duties left you familiar with blood magic?"

"They did, my lord," he answered, though it was hard to speak past the lump in his throat. Suddenly, it all connected. All the secrets, all the misery. These men were planning a weapon even greater than serosine, and they didn't care who they killed doing it. He felt an ache creeping up his spine, but he ignored it.

"I…don't want to speak out of turn," he continued slowly, "but I trust you are familiar with the…*requirements* of such magic?"

Every zinc lord knew the basics. After all, they had their own rituals. Their swords were filled with the blood of the fallen, the cobalt embedded in the sacred blades allowing each memory to pass into their minds. But serosine was nothing but a shield, preventing magic from reaching its bearer. If you truly wanted to teach a blade to cancel magic, it would need the blood of your enemies. Did they think Masked Ones grew on trees? More importantly, did they think one would come to Deyn without an army at their back?

"Blood from Zenn," the Lord of the Third said from the king's left. "It is a delicate thing, true, but we hoped to use a more…approachable Zennan. Someone more readily available. Do you think such a thing could work?"

"I…don't know," Serimh said, tilting his head. For the first time, these men had strayed from politics and into science. They said all Zennan food was powerfully magic, true. But if that were the case, then why were there so few Masked Ones? The food was sold for an ungodly price, so as far as he knew, no one had ever experimented with it. "I suppose it's possible. If you had a serosine blade, you could certainly try it."

"There is such a blade," the king said.

He shouldn't have been surprised, of course. Even though he'd asked them to tell him what they were doing with the serosine, it was no surprise they'd gone ahead on their own.

"Let us handle the Zennan," Lord Stal said. "If we get you the blood, can you fix it to the blade?"

"It would need to be fresh," Serimh said, the pit in his stomach returning. "But I'm no butcher, my lord. I'd need a Zennan and a knight to help me."

"Very well," the king said. "You'll have whatever you need. Just ready yourself, priest."

With that, his escort was back at his side, clearly taking the king's words as a dismissal. He bowed again, turning to go as he stepped back into the morning light of the hall. But before the doors closed, the council started chattering again, and he thought he heard the word *"Vindeista."* It might not just be a war with Zenn they were after, but with the Deynen guilds themselves.

He followed the knights down the stairs. None of them spoke, all their jibes seeming to fall away under the weight of what they'd just heard. He felt as hollow as the bare stone, like it was his own blood already spilt at the king's feet. He'd do it, of course. He'd learned long ago he had no limits when it came to securing his future, his *science*. But he knew the truth now for certain. War *was* coming, and he needed to see himself freed before the world caved in beneath him.

15

14ᵗʰ of Selomira 979
Rule of the Vindeista
(16ᵗʰ of Perat-kam, 985, 23ʳᵈ Year of Iron)

Chir made his way through the stands, looking for his seat through the crowd of guild members. It seemed the audience had doubled from the last fight, the smithies emptying out as everyone came to watch Sonote. The whispers had doubled too, of course, though most grew quiet as he passed. Unfortunately, there were more than enough rumors about *piabbelt*, but he wasn't worried. Sonote could fight two. Hell, he could fight ten if he wanted to. With his ferocity, his wind, and his sword, there was no one in the Zamaks with even half his skill.

He finally found his seat, nodding at the men next to him. The man smiled — at least proving not everyone was perfectly aligned with the king. Still, Sonote was going for a lordship today, and that meant their enemies would only grow. Even worse, having to cut down Lord Stal's son all but guaranteed the Council would be against them. It was one thing to climb into the mountains to slay a beast, but another thing entirely once the beast noticed your sword in its side.

He spared a glance for the king's box. Iremi nal Miri looked out at the arena, his face expressionless, his gauntleted hands folded in front of him. Was it strange for him to watch Sonote climb through the ranks as he had? If there was talk of *piabbelt*, then the council was clearly already nervous. But they couldn't afford to slow down now. He and Sonote had spent years planning for this day, and they'd agreed long ago to fight in every open duel until the job was done.

Finally, after an eternity of waiting, Sonote finally appeared with the man he'd challenged. The crown stewards closed the gates, the squire rising from the king's box with his scroll.

"On this day, the 14ᵗʰ of Selomira, Sonote nir Chiremir, grandson of guild voter Chir nir Chiremir, has challenged Tokob nal Nydin for his rank of lord."

Chir stood with his fist to his chest. The boys drew their swords, though Tokob paused, lifting his blade in the air.

"To defend the honor of our wise council, I ask the king for *piabbelt!*"

There it was. The entire stadium turned toward the king, though you wouldn't know it from the man's face. He looked as stern as ever, almost dismissive as he waved a hand, allowing the request.

"Piabbelt is granted," the squire called down. "Who will be your second, Lord Nydin?"

"I will!" came a yell from the ranks of the Zamaks where they sat beneath the king. Already in plate, the gold lion on his shoulder named him Lotre nal Romhan. He drew his blade, marching through the gap forming in the crowd as he jumped to the sand below. He walked across the arena, not sparing a glance for Sonote as he joined Nydin, the three forming a deadly triangle in the sand.

"And who will join Sonote nir Chiremir?" the squire asked, though the entire stadium already knew the answer. No one stood, the place silent save for the wind coming over the mountains.

"Do you yield or fight?" the squire finally asked.

"I fight!" Sonote yelled, raising his sword over his head to match Nydin.

Chir's heart began to pound as the squire called the start of the duel. They'd known *piabbelt* was a possibility, of course, so he wasn't too worried yet. Sonote had trained his entire life, and he had sparred against as many as five. Even against a lord, with *Vandraeb,* what could two opponents do to him?

Sonote didn't wait to find out, whipping his blade as a massive gale cut the air, dividing his two opponents. As the dust began to clear, Sonote was already running up on the right, rushing for Nydin. The boy tried to whip wind of his own back at Sonote, but the silver in *Vandraeb* cut the air as if it was nothing more than a ribbon. When he was ten feet away, Sonote leapt into the air, spinning with a fresh gale aimed at both his opponents. He—

The wind…*stopped*, dying as it left his sword, the air suddenly horrifyingly still.

Chir was immediately on his feet, staring down into the sand. Something was wrong. *Very wrong.*

Nydin dropped his cloak, revealing two metal bracers on his shoulders. They shimmered in the morning sun, their shine too perfect to be steel. They cast a sickening rainbow light, one Chir hadn't seen since the war — *serosine.*

Sonote froze, putting his sword up in a guarding stance. Chir turned toward the king, staring at the statue of a man. *Piabbelt* wasn't enough? The dogs! They were so afraid of Sonote they were willing to spit in the faces of the gods? The king didn't turn to face him, but the stadium grew quiet. But what could he do? Once a duel started, the only way to end it was to yield, losing your own place in the Zamaks. Even if this was an affront to everything he stood for, it wasn't illegal. Dishonorable, yes, but when had the bastards in the little tower ever had honor? Still, could Sonote face this? Was it even worth trying?

He turned back to face his grandson, his chest heaving. He opened his mouth to shout for the boy to yield when Sonote spun, blasting a massive wave of wind in all directions. It seemed his choice was to fight. Chir fell to the bench more than sat, his fists clenched as he watched, forcing his eyes open through the dust.

As the air cleared, Sonote's opponents were already on top of him, their swords flashing.

Sonote didn't panic, keeping his form as he held the men back. He alternated between them, swinging hard enough to keep them on the back foot, anything to force them to defend even as they tried to surround him. Still, it couldn't last. He needed an opportunity to kill one of them before he got too tired to carry on.

As Sonote pushed Romhan back again, the knight suddenly backed off. He stepped back a few paces, leaving Nydin alone. Chir narrowed his eyes. How did he think to help from back there? He couldn't exactly use his wind without hitting Nydin, and it was almost unheard of to separate during *piabbelt* for that reason. Unless… *Unless you had serosine.*

Chir's stomach dropped as Romhan swung his sword, the air seeming to groan as it shifted. The stadium's windmills began to spin frantically, the only warning of what was coming. The dust in the air began to pick up speed as it spun, though it seemed to *bend* around Nydin and the power of his serosine, putting all of its force into one place as it slammed into Sonote.

Sonote fell, though he rolled up quickly enough to block a heavy swing from Nydin. They traded a few more blows, but Romhan wasn't finished. He sent in gust after gust, the air buzzing with power. Sonote split most of them with the silver fork of his blade, but he was clearly growing tired, his swings becoming more sluggish.

"Yield," Chir whispered to himself. "Come on, lad, just yield."

What a fool he was to think the lords would fight fair! Had they cared for fairness when they sent his son to die in the war all those years ago? Did they have any interest in justice when they were willing to flaunt their serosine? He wanted to scream, but he didn't dare dishonor Sonote now. It was the boy's choice, wasn't it? Or was it Chir's? Would Sonote have been fighting at all without his grandfather in his ear all his life? A pit formed in his stomach, the awful truth finally settling in — he had sentenced his grandson to die.

Sonote pushed through another blast of wind, coming out in a dizzying burst of swings, storm gales leaping from *Vandraeb* as he pushed forward, seeking Nydin's neck. It was a final effort, and a desperate one, but if he dropped Nydin, he could easily deal with Romhan, serosine or not. Suddenly, time seemed to slow, the crowd going silent as they watched Sonote swing for Nydin's neck. He almost reached it, the blade coming within an inch as Romhan sent in another blast of wind.

Sonote was hit squarely in the chest, falling to his back, no longer able to roll after putting everything into that swing. Nydin didn't wait, pushing forward in an overhand swing. Sonote scrambled to one knee, catching Nydin's blade between *Vandraeb's* forks. His arms shook from the effort, raised above his head as Nydin pushed down. The other boy's eyes were huge behind his helmet, crazed and full of bloodlust as he tried to break Sonote.

Slowly, like a ghost from the upper valleys, Romhan walked over.

"No," Chir whispered, biting his lip to keep from crying out.

The knight was like a sleepwalker, like he couldn't believe himself they'd really won. He stopped a foot away from the struggling men, his sword still held carefully before him.

"Yield!" Romhan shouted at Sonote.

It was a mercy compared to the dishonor they'd already done him, but suddenly Chir knew what his grandson would say. All that training, all that fighting… It had drained the joy out of that perfect boy. Chir had honed him like a blade, and a blade could only ever have one purpose.

"Never!" Sonote shouted.

Finding a last burst of strength, Sonote threw Nydin back, getting to his feet. But Romhan had already swung, his blade finding Sonote's throat in a spray of blood. Sonote twisted as he fell, and for a second, Chir could see his eyes through his helmet, a single flash of white as he crumpled to the ground.

Blood burst into Chir's mouth as he bit through his lip. He was shaking, clamping his eyes shut as the arena roared. There was no silence for his grandson, no awe like when he'd killed Stal's son. He clenched his teeth, feeling like they might crack as he forced himself to stand, the squire calling out the result of the duel. He somehow bowed to Lord Nydin, but his eyes soon found the king, the man sitting, his face completely unchanged as he looked out at Sonote's blood where it pooled against the sand. There was no emotion in that gaze. No pity, no regret. No one would dare mourn this perfect, wonderful boy. No one would even care that the kingdom had just lost its final chance at peace.

Chir fell to his knees, able to stand no more.

———

Chir found himself back at the smithy. It was dark, the sun gone. *Vandraeb* sat before him on the workbench, the blade gleaming in the darkness. He could hardly remember walking back from the arena, the day becoming a horrible, ugly blur. He had stayed in the practice room until the priests came, until he could be sure Sonote's body would be cared for in its final moments before the pyre.

His daughter-in-law would have heard by now, but he couldn't bring himself to head for home, to stand with her in her grief. Not when it was his fault… But even having seen the boy die himself, it didn't feel true. It felt like Sonote might walk in at any moment, demanding to know why he had walked off with his sword. After all, he was going to need it, wasn't he? For the next duel and for the ones after that, each rung on the ladder as he went after the king.

Chir stood, roaring as he swung the sword, knocking over a shelf of curing oils. He fell into a frenzy after that, destroying everything within reach. *Vandraeb,* so useless against the serosine, was perfectly capable of destroying a workshop. He broke shelves, split jars, even toppled the forge. He swung until he thought he might collapse, but in the end, it had done nothing. He was still stuck in this terrible place, a cursed valley where Sonote's sun would never shine again.

He crumpled to the floor, sobbing into his hands, the sword forgotten at his side. But even as he struggled to catch his breath, his mind drowning in sorrow, he saw the king's face in the darkness. Even as it threatened to block Sonote's, Iremi nal Miri was like a mountain, blotting out the sky.

His guild position meant nothing, the *law* meant nothing. He had held his tongue, had honored Sonote, but he was finished pretending now. There was no honor left in this basin, even for himself. The boy had given everything, and Chir had let him, foolish enough to think it would make a difference. Now, Chir was free. Free to destroy himself for his revenge. However long he had left, no matter what it took from him, he would see the zinc lords dead.

16

15ᵗʰ of Selomira 979
Rule of the Vindeista
(17ᵗʰ of Perat-kam, 985, 23ʳᵈ Year of Iron)

Eyri walked past the lake, her mind brimming with ideas of what the day could bring. How long had it been since she'd actually been excited like this? The feeling had certainly been rare as a Masked One. Even so, her time in Deyn felt like it had been marked only by a crushing weight, each day marred by her uselessness. Now, she was finally getting closer, climbing back up the mountain of who she was meant to be. She'd spent so much time wondering about what she'd done in the temple, about why she'd felt the gods so clearly only to have them stripped away from her. But maybe this was why. So she could be here for this moment.

Chir had given her the day before off for the duels, but she'd come to the Zinc Quarter anyway, looking for odd jobs she could do. She still owed the farmer's guild a workday for Teros's school, of course, but after she'd gotten so close to the forge, it felt wrong to be banished to some field, especially with the knights away at the arena. She'd eventually found someone — possibly one of only a dozen still working during the duels — who let her move some boxes.

She'd listened to the roars of the stadium while she worked, memorizing every detail she could — the streets, the hill to the central city, the forge. Without the normal buzz of activity, it had been easier to track the routes the guards used on patrol. She'd finally been sent home as people streamed out of the arena, though she never saw Chir and Sonote. Had they won, carried off to feast with the knights? She certainly hoped so. Even as the serosine boiled her blood, Chir seemed like a kind person. Besides, as Viden always said, most men didn't ask for war. You didn't blame the snake's tail for biting you, you just took the head off.

Thinking of Viden made her pause, looking back toward the west where Zenn was hidden beyond the horizon. Had he died yet? He must have. She thought of him often, especially on the nights she couldn't sleep, wishing she'd been there to hold his hand at the end. She hoped they hadn't punished him for what she'd done. But even more, she…hoped he was proud of her still. The fight in the temple had gone against everything she'd ever been taught, but he'd told her himself to run, hadn't he? He'd seen something in her, something human, and abandoned by the gods or not, she couldn't ever wear the mask again.

She reached the smithy, but the doors and windows were closed. Chir had said he started early, but had he gone out instead, celebrating after the duel? Unfortunately, she and Teros wouldn't survive without pay, so she had no choice but to wait for him. She turned, about to sit against the wall when she heard something from inside the shop. It was a scratching sound, like a rat clawing at a cupboard.

Was there an animal in there? She hadn't seen any food the day before, but that didn't mean a rat couldn't ruin his equipment. She pushed the door, and to her surprise, it creaked open. As light flooded the room, though, all she found Chir, facedown with his white hair sticking out. She thought he might be dead, but then she realized where the sound came from. He held Sonote's sword limply at his side, slowly circling in his hand as it scratched against the stone floor.

"Chir?" she asked, staying by the doorway. "Are you alright?"

He looked up, his eyes red.

"Eyri," he said slowly, as if he'd forgotten who she was. He looked around at the storeroom, and she followed his eyes, finally noticing that everything had been destroyed.

"What happened?" she asked, moving for a broom in the corner, but he stopped her.

"Sonote's dead."

"He's…dead?" she asked, a chill crawling up her spine.

It seemed impossible. As much death as she'd seen, the boy had still seemed so…*solid,* like a stone in the waste, untouchable, unbreakable. And what did that mean for her? How would she fight a crown that could kill a knight so easily?

"I'm—" she started, but Chir groaned, dropping his head back to the table.

"Just come back tomorrow. We'll have orders to do then."

"I—"

"Tomorrow," he said again.

She walked quietly to the door, shutting it behind her. A man at the smithy across the street gave her a look before turning away, shaking his head. Perhaps she could work with the farmer's guild after all… She headed back toward the lake, suddenly eager to be away. But what of the serosine? She stopped in the middle of the street, but a knight walked by, glaring at her.

Was working with Chir a liability now? She glanced toward the forge. He was still her only way inside, but maybe it really would be best to leave for the day. After all, if people recognized her as his assistant now, today would be a day full of gossip. She clenched her hands, sucking in a deep breath. Even with her heart already brimming with hatred for Deyn, she found a fresh reserve.

How could they have done this to Chir? To Sonote?

Perhaps she should have allied herself with them, found a way to help them win their duels, but it was too late for that now. Besides, they'd never help her if they knew what she was up to. She would simply have to stick to the plan and hope destroying the zinc king would bring Chir a bit of solace. She walked on, trying to avoid the eyes watching her from all the smithies. As she left the quarter, though, she found herself looking over her shoulder, suddenly afraid the place might swallow her whole.

———

Teros leaned forward on the ground, carefully pulling a wet brush across the stones as he drew the words the teacher told them to. He was sitting in a line with the others in the shade of the guild hall, almost finished with their first lesson. They were arranged by age, so he was next to Liska, while Si'tar was at the other end, working on easier words.

"That's not bad," Liska said, leaning over to look at the words he'd drawn. Their group was working on the names of the Elders — the Deynen ones, anyway — and the Deynen letters were hard to write.

"Really?" Teros asked, looking at Liska's. Hers looked like they should have been done in ink and framed. He'd learned quickly that she was good at basically everything, but instead of making him feel bad, it made him feel strangely hopeful — like he could do anything too if he set his mind to it. And even though his letters were still blocky, he was leaning twice as fast now that he was at the school.

"Again," the teacher said, and they all shifted, crawling across the stone to the top where there were fresh dry spots to work on. The wind blew constantly across the fields, drying the water as the air was warmed by the massive cobalt spikes on the north end of the village. He could see men moving in the distance, preparing for the spring planting.

As they began another round of writing, the teacher went back into the guild house to work with the others. It was almost Baker's Day, and the adults were frantically preparing their grain for sale. The kids would be helping soon too, but they were still allowed to do their lessons on their breaks.

It was so…refreshing compared to how he'd always done things. Ever since he was little, he'd always done just one thing at a time. But life in the village had so much more variety. You got to study, but you also got to work, never staying on one task for too long. It made him think of days with Mother, when she'd free him from his tutors so they could do whatever they liked around the farm.

"Together," he whispered to himself, shutting his eyes in the middle of a word. Still, he felt happy. Things were good now, and it was easier to keep the bad faces from his mind. Learning about the people of this basin, it felt like he was finally doing what he was meant to. Uncle Elin had always said the Mother's Valley ought to be united, and maybe, learning Deynen, he could help with that. Even if Eyri was wrong and they never made it home, it had to matter that they made a life here. He—

"You're doing it again," Liska said, nudging him.

"Sorry?" Teros asked, quickly opening his eyes. Had he whispered out loud? He'd meant to do it in his mind, but it was hard to remember the difference sometimes.

"Don't be," she said, going back to her letters. "Just be careful. I told the others you were praying like the Zennans do, but if you do it too much, they'll just keep thinking you're a *spo'gimes.*"

"You don't pray?" he asked.

"We do," she said, gesturing around the village. "In Deyn, we work to pray. It honors the Snow Father."

He looked around at the adults scattered throughout the square. Like a pond teeming with fish, they all dashed about doing different things. Some pulled sleds full of grain from the storehouse to the mill while others filled bags with finished flour. The women in the guild house were sewing new bags together and others were piling finished ones back in the storehouse for merchants to come get. Soon, the children would help to count them, and in the afternoon, they'd move on to assisting with the planting.

"Yeah, I guess so," he said.

Liska smiled at him, and they went back to writing their words. He clenched his teeth, trying to keep his tongue from whispering out loud. He'd never been caught doing it before, and it made his neck hot with shame. It was a wonder Liska didn't think him strange — a wonder anyone tolerated him at all. But what was he to do? He could feel the whispers jumping around in his head like tadpoles, and he needed to do something before the bad faces came swimming back to the surface. Still, if he was going to be around people again, he couldn't whisper all the time...

He finished his last word, quietly looking around the village again. He looked at the mountains, the dark stone reaching into the sky. He traced them with his eyes, their faces dotted with moss. He tried to imagine the entire stretch of the mountains in his mind's eye, picturing how the stone wrapped around them, embracing the valley. He pictured himself from above, like a bird, sitting in that safe, protected place. It felt like he could feel every bit of beauty pouring into him, and suddenly, he felt better. The voices disappeared. He was safe, and he and everything around him were...*together.*

"Hey, isn't that your Mehm?" Liska asked, breaking into his dream. For a moment, he thought she meant Mother, as if his beautiful thoughts had brought her spirit back from Sen'el'seng.

He blinked, following her eyes to find Eyri walking into the village. His heart dropped, feeling exactly like he had the first time she'd caught him. Had he done something wrong? Was she here to take him back to the cave?

As he watched, though, she didn't come toward him, going straight up to the guild boss. She gestured with her hands, looking like she was lifting something. The man nodded, pointing to the workers who were carrying finished bags of grain back to the storehouses. She bowed, finally turning in Teros's direction.

She smiled, waving as she walked away to work.

"She seems nice," Liska said, going back to her writing. "At least when she isn't catching you sneaking off. Is she a good Mehm?"

"She…" Teros started, trailing off. He suddenly felt even worse than he had when Eyri arrived. She had done so much to take care of him, and he wasn't appreciating her at all. What if he lost her like Mother? "She's a great Mehm. She works really hard."

"No greater honor to the Snow Father," Liska said, nodding her approval. "Especially if she made the time to do her guild work on top of finding rocks. Has she found any yet?"

"She said she's close," Teros said, watching Eyri as she worked. Liska was referring to his lie, of course, when he'd pretended Eyri had moved him to the mountains for geology. But what would happen when she really found the serosine? Could she destroy it on her own? He ought to help her, but he was useless without the Principles. He was afraid for her, and…if he was honest with himself, he was afraid to give up his life in Hv'rano too. It left him caught between two awful choices — hoping she succeeded and hoping she didn't. The second, though, was full of guilt, threatening to rip his heart free from his chest as the whispers came flooding back, his stomach clenching with fear.

"Alright, children," the teacher said, reappearing. "Get ready to learn another set of words and then we'll do some work."

He picked his brush back up, but the stone suddenly looked impossibly empty, like it could never hold the words he wanted to write, no matter how hard he tried. He tried to look over his shoulder for Eyri, to at least follow her with his eyes. But he couldn't find her, and the image he'd painted of the valley in his mind was suddenly broken open, the two halves of his mind turning into a chasm.

"Together," he whispered, quiet enough he hoped that Liska wouldn't hear.

17

19ᵗʰ of Selomira 979
Rule of the Vindeista
(21ˢᵗ of Perat-kam, 985, 23ʳᵈ Year of Iron)

Serimh hurried through the workshop, sweat dripping from his brow. He clutched a dozen vials to his chest, the glass warm to the touch from where they'd been nestled in the fire. A strange smell wafted up from the blood within, like an old rusty kettle. He couldn't afford to trip with his hands full of glass, of course, but neither could he wait. Nearly a week of experiments had led to nothing, and it was only a matter of time before his keepers grew tired of his failure — and his use of their blood.

It was best not to think too hard on where they'd gotten that blood, of course. The knights kept their own reserves in a cave near the mountains — a priest could heal you much more effectively if they had a bit of your own blood for their cobalt casings — but surely the knights weren't giving him their own blood with war so close at hand. Hopefully it was from a…benign source, like the monthly bleeding of the tower's serving women or something like that. Unfortunately, there were a thousand ways to get what you needed in Deyn, especially for men as ruthless as the zinc lords.

He placed the vials into twelve separate holders, each one about a foot apart and directly in front of a smooth iron plate. It was a painstaking process and far from an exact one, completely in the realm of, well…*magic*. There were priests who spent their entire lives studying the craft, but it wasn't as if Iremi nal Miri could walk up to the temple and ask for their help — not if he wanted to keep the war he was planning secret.

Unfortunately, secrecy seemed to be the only thing the knights *did* understand. They'd finally forced him from the central tower, moving him into the Zinc Quarter. He spared a glance out the window of his new workshop, the deathly quiet of the empty arena the only thing visible through the narrow castle window. He would miss his old view — and the slow study he'd been making of the sacred pillars — but it hardly mattered now.

Even if he felt like he was slowly inching toward the secrets of the gods, it wasn't like anyone else had ever cared about his research. The priests had never come to his rescue, and neither had his father's artifelians. He still wanted to uncover the secrets of the gods, desperately so, but as a man of science, he also had to face facts. He was alone, and if he wanted his life back, he'd have to free himself.

Thankfully, even if he was a novice with blood magic, there was no one who knew more about the Snow Father than he did. And just like when he'd discovered cobalt spikes for farming all those years ago, Serimh had gone back to the Elder's journals, digging through the man's memories for answers.

The Snow Father, Arikai nol D'ek, had been a blacksmith in the Giant Lands. Perhaps that was why he'd sought the chilly mountains of Deyn, eager to reestablish the mines he'd been forced to abandon in the realm of the gods. But why the Zinc Father had followed with his knights was still a mystery. Had they simply wanted to stay close to their blacksmith? Or had the Snow Father promised them magic for their blades, knowing he could use the sacred pillars for his forge?

Whatever the reason, it hardly mattered now. They had found Deyn's black waterfalls and decided to stay, oblivious to the pain awaiting them. Winter had arrived much sooner than they'd expected, dumping snow over the basin. Unfortunately, nol D'ek's journals grew brief during that first winter. But how had he let it happen? If the Elders were truly blessed by the Sacred Mother, wouldn't she have warned them? Why not send them somewhere else? Unless she *had* warned them, and Arikai nol D'ek had stayed anyway…

At any rate, every Deynen knew how those bitter months had ended. On the Day of Loss, the cold at its most bitter, Arikai nol D'ek's wife had died, succumbing to the snow he'd forced her into. He'd turned her into a statue — the same one still gracing the tip of the glacier — but not before draining her blood. He'd taken that blood and bound it to every ounce of iron they'd brought from the Giant Lands, starting a blaze of Passion so intense it burned until the Day of Joy, when the start of spring had finally signaled their survival. Now, Serimh would follow in the man's footsteps — assuming he didn't fail for the hundredth bloody time…

With all the vials in place, he moved from plate to plate, spreading a drop from each into a perfect circle on the iron. Growing up, the Snow Father's treatment of his wife's blood had always struck him as macabre. That was, of course, until his own mother had died, and Father had worn her blood around his neck, putting a drop in every artifel in their house. People did funny things when they mourned, and Serimh was no exception. Even if he was only mourning the career they'd stripped from him, selling your soul for your freedom certainly couldn't come from anywhere but the deepest grief.

With the blood in place, he placed a weighted gold disc on top of each circle, the metal seeming to hum as it began to react. Iron was supposedly the strongest base you could use, bonding with what must have been an abundance of the metal already in the blood. Still, blood seemed to have dozens of metals in it, and none of the Elder's writings explained why gold was so important to the bonding process.

As the humming reached its peak, he placed candles on top of the gold discs, moving as quickly as he could so he could light them all. The iron plates immediately burst into flame — the workbench thankfully made of stone — as the blood brought out the Passion in the iron, allowing the metal to burn like wood as it enhanced its power. And the flames were...*all different.*

Serimh sighed, slumping onto his stool. The flames were still hot, but he didn't care, dropping his forehead on the workbench. It simply couldn't be his fault. There had been some wobbles at the start, true, but he was a man of science, and he'd perfected his methods, treating each blood sample completely identically. It had to be the blood itself, some impurity between each sample changing the blend of metals. He couldn't know for certain, of course, not without the knights telling him where they bloody got it from.

Perhaps it didn't matter. While his flames weren't yet identical, he *had* gotten to the point of consistently bonding metal with blood. More importantly, when he treated the serosine, he'd presumably be working off of a single Zennan subject — gods forbid they were bold enough to kidnap more than one. Still, that would only give him four to six liters of blood to work with — assuming they didn't waste any. Would it be enough to treat a hundred pounds of serosine?

He got up, going back to the cobalt chest in the corner. It glowed blue from its artifels, the glass vials of blood inside like sapphires. They'd only given him a few ounces from each candidate, but suppose he tried to use just one person's sample to get a uniform flame? Unfortunately, they didn't have any serosine to spare — hence his experiments with iron — but he'd have to do his best with what he had. Iron burned, and serosine cancelled magic. He'd just have to hope the final reaction was to his captors' liking.

He looked back out at the arena, taking a deep breath. As the sun rose above Sen'el'tul, the iron glowed red, as if it were covered in blood. Was it a vision of the future? If war came again, it wouldn't be long until the entire basin was filled with death. Unfortunately, it wasn't his place to question the lords of this godsforsaken land. He was a man of science, and it was his job to pick up the pieces, to make sure there was something left when the fires went out.

18

Eyri slowly poured molten metal into a mold, ignoring the blazing heat on her face. Chir sat behind her, silent as he stared through the open door. When she'd returned a few days earlier, he'd cleaned the shop, replacing everything he'd broken. He then gave her a list of instructions and orders to be fulfilled before he sat, unmoving. Each day he was sitting there when she arrived, and he was still there when she left each night. Hopefully he was eating and sleeping, though he didn't look it. There were heavy bags under his eyes, and he'd lost what little weight he'd had to spare.

It seemed like the only thing in the world to him was the door, as if he were waiting for Sonote to walk through it, to apologize for making him worry. As Eyri submerged the mold in the dark black water, making it hiss, Chir finally moved. He still worked the anvil — something that would likely take her years to figure out — fixing the final edges of the blades, tongs, and hinges they made each day.

She stood behind him, watching as he pounded the metal with a hammer. He didn't waste a single motion, each movement perfectly precise. They were making a sickle today, an order from the farmer's guild. Still, detached from the handle, it was hard to see it as anything but a sword. Its curved blade would cut a neck as easily as wheat, especially with Chir giving it such a fine edge. She glanced toward the door, Sonote's sword now hung above the entryway, waiting for his return.

She didn't know what to say to him in his grief. When she'd been in the tower, there was death all around — Masked Ones succumbing to the Passing, dying in the field, killing each other in duels not unlike Sonote's. But for them, death had simply been a fact. You slept in your own room and put on your own mask. There were no blank spaces when someone died, no empty doorframes to stare through. You just…moved on.

But that was 732. What about Eyri? She'd lost her brother, hadn't she? Even as she'd been forced to look ahead — to keep Teros alive, to keep food on the table, to get them back home — she felt the weight in her heart. In fact, working like an ox from sunup to sundown, Borash felt like the only thing — other than Teros — reminding her of who she really was. Even if she didn't know that person all that well…

She sucked in a breath, setting her jaw. Maybe she didn't know who she was, but if she had any chance of finding out, she needed to find the serosine and free them of this place. Even if she felt bad for Chir, she had to push him. It had been days since she'd been sent on any type of errand, and even if they were running low on cesium, the man only had eyes for the next project on his list. She needed him to look ahead, to use her to get what he needed — and get her to the serosine.

"Are there…many more jobs coming in?" she asked.

Chir froze, the hammer held high in the air. She almost shifted her stance, sure he'd turn and swing it at her, if only to silence the intrusion on his grief.

"Sorry," he said, swinging the hammer again before putting it to the side. He inspected the sickle's blade quickly before returning it to the fire for the next round of honing.

"It's the strangest thing," he said, sighing. He put his back to the forge, folding his arms. "I almost forgot how to speak Zennan. When you spoke, it felt like the words couldn't reach me." He shook his head. "What were you saying?"

"I was just wondering how many more jobs you have," she said. "We're…running out of supplies."

He looked at his shelves — the one's he'd pounded into dust just a week earlier — his eyes scanning the jars as if he could see inside them.

"I suppose we must be," he said, nodding. He pinched his forehead before finally meeting her eyes. "We have more jobs than ever. They're pouring in."

His eyes drifted to the left, to where the arena was hiding beyond the walls of the smithy.

"It's what those dogs do. They try to buy you, as if you could forget what you've lost."

She watched him, a deep sadness coming over her. It felt too similar to her time in the mask, the differences between her and Chir falling away. She couldn't stop her next words from leaving her mouth.

"Why not stop? Why not leave the guild?"

He met her eyes. His were like a glacier, a piercing color she'd only ever seen in Deyn. It felt like he was seeing her for the first time since the duel. Somehow, he smiled.

"And go where, child? I still have a daughter-in-law to feed. Besides, you can't get revenge if you drop your blade."

Revenge… Suppose he might be willing to help her? Suppose he wanted to make the knights pay? He— *No.* She could trust no one. Surely he didn't mean it the way she wished he did. Trust would only get her killed.

"I think we've done quite enough for the day," he said, breaking the spell as he glanced at the clock. He pulled some money from his pocket, pressing it into her hand.

"Why don't you run along to your son? It's good to spend time with family while you have them."

She nodded, turning to go. She was in no position to refuse money for her work, even if he was grief-stricken.

"I'll see you tomorrow," she said. But as she crossed through the open doorway, she couldn't help but look at Sonote's sword again. What made her different from that boy? What made her think she would fare any better against the knights?

She bought enough food for a feast from the merchants who worked the outskirts of the Zinc Quarter, slinging it over her shoulder as she made her way back to the cave. It wasn't as if Chir had given her a fortune — two siulken — but after a months of only making a handful of rusts each day, twenty siulkiy worth of coin *felt* like a fortune. She'd been able to buy a whole chicken, vegetables, and a dozen eggs, all with about eight of the smaller coins left over.

Still, as excited as she was to finally feed Teros properly, she couldn't get Sonote's sword out of her mind. Looking at that wicked blade above the door all day, it only made her think of her own hidden in the cave. She'd wielded hers a lot longer than Sonote had — and had buried it in the necks of a half-dozen knights besides — but was it still sharp enough for what lay ahead? She quickened her pace, suddenly eager to be home. She needed to feel the sword in her hand, to practice her forms before she forgot them.

As she came over the ridge and started down into the valley, the wind picked up. She imagined it was the wind of a zinc knight's sword. She tried to follow the currents of Identity in her mind — even if it was nearly impossible after this many months without any sacred food from Zenn. She moved her feet to the wind's rhythm, snaking back and forth along the path, imagining the way she would swing her sword.

It felt like she had wasted so much time since coming here. She still had no answer for where her magic had gone, and she'd spent so many days just scraping by she hadn't practiced at all outside of teaching Teros. Suppose she found the serosine and even managed to destroy it, did she really think she was strong enough to escape alive? She wouldn't mind dying to pay for her crimes, but what of her boy? He seemed to like his school, his life here, but if she died, she'd never return him home, never be able to give him what he deserved. He—

She saw Teros ahead, coming up the path from the village toward the mountains. He was normally home before her, but with Chir letting her go early, it seemed their schedules had lined up for once. She waved, but he wasn't looking, his eyes on the ground ahead of him as he mumbled to himself. She looked over her shoulder, feeling a flash of anger. Why couldn't he pay attention? Who knew how many people walked the road to Hv'rano during the day? What if he wasn't looking and they wondered why a boy was walking alone into the mountains?

"Teros," she said more sharply than she meant to.

He looked up, and she found herself wincing, the pained look on his face the exact same as the one he'd given her when she first found him in the village.

"You…need to watch the road," she said more gently, swallowing as bile climbed into her throat. All he did in return was nod, his eyes still wide, so she waved him over, taking him by the shoulder as they turned onto the mountain path.

"I got paid today," she said, "there's lots of food."

"Thank you," he said quietly, his eyes still on the ground.

She almost chided him again, but why not let him look wherever he wanted when she was there to protect him? Assuming she *could* protect him… It only made her think of that sword again, but she pushed the thought away. She ought to enjoy the little time she had with Teros; it wasn't often they got to be together in the evenings. She sucked in a breath, forcing a smile to her face.

"Any guesses for what I bought?"

He finally looked up, glancing over her shoulder where her bag was strung.

"Clams?" he asked.

"Well, it's not *clams,*" she said, laughing. She tousled his hair. "They're out of season, and from Pen'dil Sing besides. Guess again."

How did she know a thing like that? She hadn't ever eaten anything besides her rations in the tower. She must have heard the other Masked Ones talk about it over the years. But maybe that was a good thing; maybe she knew more about being a person than she thought.

It took him two more guesses — and a bit of clucking from her — but Teros finally figured out what was in the bag. More importantly, she actually got him to laugh too, and by the time they reached their cave, he was babbling about all the ways he might prepare the bird.

For a while, she *did* enjoy the evening. She used her knife to help dress the chicken, and she sat with Teros while he cooked, listening as he told her about school. She even told him a story of her own, about the time Viden had cooked a crow for her during the war, not even twenty miles from where they were now. But as the fire burned low, the stars appearing overhead, she started to think about her sword again. It seemed to call for her from the its hiding place by their bed, begging to be held, to be drawn.

Finally, as Teros yawned for the dozenth time, she dragged him to bed, tucking him in beneath her cloak.

"Won't you come to bed too?" he asked, gripping her hand.

She knew he had trouble sleeping without her, his muttering always at its worst just after he fell asleep. But she couldn't join him, not when she knew she'd only see the sword when she closed her eyes.

"I can sit for a minute, but I have my own practicing to do." Still, she still leaned in, kissing his forehead as she remembered her own Mems doing. "Just try to sleep; I'll be right outside."

"Okay," he said, frowning, but he closed his eyes, and after only a few minutes, his tiny hand in hers, he fell asleep, his breathing deep.

She took the sword, creeping out of the cave. The moon was above the cavern, making its impossibly short trip over their crack in the rock. But for the moment, everything was bathed in blue light. She stood there, staring at the sword in her hand. Slowly, she pulled it free, the blade glittering in the darkness, its silvery amalgam like the moon itself. When was the last time she actually drew her sword, let it see the light it so clearly yearned for?

She dropped into a low stance, letting go of the scabbard as she moved into her sword forms. Soon, she began to sweat despite the cool of the night, but it felt...*incredible.* She felt like herself again, her muscles eager to do anything but ache, anything more than the drudgery her life had been swallowed by. She moved like a dancer, her sword a ribbon of light as it flickered under the moon.

She went on like that for a long time, until her back was slick with sweat. Still, the night air kept her cool, and she pushed on, savoring the breeze rushing through the pass. As she danced through her forms, she realized she *could* feel the wind. Suddenly, strands of Identity appeared before her eyes. She had gone so long without the magic, it felt like a trick of the eye. Still, she didn't dare question it further, darting between the currents, swinging her sword to the rhythm of the wind.

She knew then that she could fight the zinc lords. Whatever she was now, some part of her still clung to the gods. Even if they'd abandoned her in this waste, she'd known their touch, and she could see the secrets of their world. She began to fight *against* the wind, imagining the streaks of Identity were sent from a zinc knight's blade. She twisted and jumped, rolling and swinging as she fought her shadow foe.

It didn't last long. Eventually, the wind became just wind again. Still, she'd definitely seen it, hadn't she? Something in her sword had brought Identity back to her, even if she'd never maintain it without the sacred food. She stood there, drenched with sweat, her lungs heaving as she listened to the steady sound of the cave, like breathing. She didn't know if she could give Teros the life he deserved, didn't know when she would find the serosine. She didn't even know if such a thing would absolve her of her crimes. But she finally knew what she was. She wasn't a Masked One. She was a blade, and she would fight until the wind stopped blowing.

19

**40ᵗʰ of Sund-z'ar, 970, 8ᵗʰ Year of Iron
15ᵗʰ Day of the War - 'The Day of the Hawk'
Fifteen Years Ago**

Viden stared out at the line of barren hills, waiting for signs of movement. He held his message bottle tightly in his hand, ready to send it off with a flare of Place at a moment's notice. The western flats outside Deyn looked much like the wilds outside Zenn — barren. Still, the rocky slopes were anything but empty, random chasms and boulders offering ample opportunities for the enemy to hide. There was a steady breeze coming from the north, but he smelt only dust.

Behind him, he heard the steady thwack-thwack-thwack of Curan throwing her blade into a clump of moss. She was getting mighty good with the knife, already able to hit a point no larger than a fuller. She was also constantly asking him to spar, the promise of the duels having apparently caught her eye. Assuming he could keep her alive through this bloody war, there was no doubt everyone would remember his little girl — and the number 732.

"Most people try to miss once in a while," he said without turning around to hide his smile. "Keeps the blade from going dull."

"Doesn't take much of a blade to take an eye," Curan said with a grunt as she threw again, the blade making its predictable thud into the moss a moment later. Still, she took a break, pulling her knife free as she came up next to him.

"Still nothing?" she asked, scanning the hills.

"No, lad," he said, putting his arm around her. He couldn't always risk being so informal with his daughter, but the army's lithium lines stretched for dozens of miles, and the nearest outpost was beyond the next rise. "You don't have to be so eager to fight, you know. You'll show your mettle soon enough."

"Not much point in being at war if we don't get to do anything."

He laughed. "First zinc knights we see, I'll let you have the biggest one."

There was no point in dashing her hopes, but if he had anything to say about it, she'd see very little of the action. Luckily, the Zi'yun brigades — and their lithium lines — still had plenty of important work to do. Once their wagon train had arrived, they'd gotten their numbers back up to nearly 250 masks, pushing the zinc lot back to a big crack in the earth called Sesarin, some ten miles west of Deyn. Now the army was massing their troops, waiting on the king to attack. With the king's son, Prince Bitan, to the north and the Cobalt Duke to the south, he'd gotten them stationed at the far end of the line — and hopefully out of harm's way. That was, assuming he could keep Curan from taking matters into her own hands…

He'd trained her religiously back in Zenn, desperate to coat her in a shield of excellence. He'd seen plenty of scrapes in his career, and sometimes, the only way to make sure you didn't get killed in their line of work was to do the killing. Unfortunately, all his training had *worked,* and now he had a little blade on his hands, all too eager do what blades did best.

"I just want to protect Zenn," Curan said quietly, her eyes still glued to the horizon.

Of course, it wasn't *just* training… He hugged her tighter, letting out a sigh. More than anyone he'd ever seen wear the mask, this girl was obsessed with loyalty. To her country — to her family. She didn't think of finding them, thankfully — though there'd been a handful of Masked Ones put down for that. She thought only to protect them with her service. Even if everything the king said about this war and guarding the basin was bollocks, the girl's heart, at least, was true. She really believed this war mattered, and it only mattered because she wanted to protect her kin.

"I know, lad," he said. "And you are. These message lines are the only thing holding this army together. You stick with me, and we'll save our basin yet. We—"

He paused, noticing something on the horizon.

"Riders," Curan said, reaching for the spy glass on the ground between them. "Send the message!"

"Not yet," he said, squinting between the hills. There was a pair of horses darting between the slopes. They flew no flag, but they were obviously Deynen by their armor. "We need to know which way they're going."

Unfortunately, as he watched the outriders heading north, he learned something else — *they weren't alone.* An entire bloody company of zinc knights emerged from the pass, all of them riding in the direction of Prince Bitan. A passel of hawks circled overhead, no doubt about to give away their position.

"We need to go."

Viden took his message bottle, turning the dials near the top to indicate how many enemies were moving in which direction. Then he flared Place, the bottle disappearing from his hand as it moved up the lithium line. He felt the Passing rear its ugly head, but he ignored it. Place wasn't as bad as the others, and besides, Curan would need him another ten years yet. He wasn't about to start losing his head over a little bit of death in his blood.

Nearly out of lithium, he swallowed another vial of dandelion, ignoring the bitter taste as hundreds of anchors appeared in his mind. They stretched all the way across the front, though the nearer ones burned brightest. They needed to head south, to tell the duke to send help. Bitan didn't have nearly enough men to hold their flank. But more importantly, he wanted his little girl off this hill before the knights noticed them. Unfortunately, even if the Cobalt Duke was a snake, there was probably nowhere safer on the front lines than his camp.

"Hold onto me," he said, reaching for Curan's hand.

They disappeared into the waypoints, emerging in Elin nir Dek'rc's camp. Set into a rise five miles south of their previous position, the camp was in total disarray. Men were abandoning their tents, sprinting further southward — and *away* from Bitan — their weapons in hand. Viden scanned the horizon, but he couldn't see any zinc knights. He turned to Curan.

"No matter what, don't leave my side. But leave room for me to swing my sword, understood?"

She gave him a strange look but nodded. She was still too young to understand the dangers on her own side of the war. For some reason, he found himself quoting his father again.

"There's no snake in the basin that doesn't bite without warning, lad. Best not to give 'em any reason all the same."

Odd that he should still be quoting a man who sold him for grain. But with his own daughter to protect now, he found himself in desperate need of wisdom. Perhaps there wasn't much value in a bag of odd sayings, but how else could he prepare Curan for the cruel world she'd been sold into? They'd been dirt-poor, but his father *had* been wise in his own way. Even if he'd handed Viden a life of suffering, at least it had been enough to protect his sister, to—

Viden shook his head, focusing on the camp ahead. This was no time for pondering. He set off toward the duke's tent, Curan scurrying behind. Compared to the shabby woolen tents of the soldiers, the duke lived in a palace, his tent rising at least ten feet in the air with multiple wings, the wool died purple. Scouts hurried in and out with messages, and they slipped in with them, the guards at the main flap unwilling to stop a pair of Masked Ones.

Inside, dozens of people stood around a giant map-covered table. There were human soldiers, captains, and a handful of others in masks. Dek'rc stood in the center, leaning forward with his palms on the map, his little dog 151 at his side.

"My lord," Viden said, tapping Curan so she bowed with him. "We just came from the north end of the line. There's an entire of company heading for Prince Bitan. He needs reinforcements."

The room went silent, a dozen unfriendly eyes turning on them. The duke stood slowly, sparing a glance for Curan, a glance that made Viden's blood boil.

"That's not possible," the duke said. "We're heading south. There's zinc knights on all sides, bloody hawks all over."

"With all due respect, my lord, the flank—"

"The *flank*," the duke said, "is in good hands. My scouts in the east tell me the exact opposite of what you've said. They have two companies hitting the Duke of Identity just south of here. But if you'd like to check on the prince yourself, I'd be happy to hold onto your little one here…"

151's hand went to his sword, the threat all too clear. Perhaps if he'd still been alone in this world, he'd give it a go. Prince Bitan was a good man, and the world would certainly be better off without 151 in it. But there was something else happening here. He'd seen that company with his own eyes. The duke was lying. As his father always said, you shouldn't bet a rich man for a fuller when he was betting with your blood. And no matter how loyal he was to the king, he realized in that moment he'd never care about anything more than his daughter. He'd let the bastards take one from him, and he wouldn't ever let it happen again. Even if he'd never forgive himself for making her a monster like he was…

"I apologize for my mistake," Viden said, bowing. "If it's all the same to you, I'd like to ride south with your men and secure the Duke of Identity."

"Good man," Dek'rc said, smiling. "We'll get you some horses."

Viden nodded, dragging Curan from the tent before those men could leer at his daughter again. No matter what, he wouldn't let her become a dog for those wicked men.

They stumbled away like men walking the mist, his eyes searching desperately for those horses. But before they made it to the first line of soldiers' tents, Curan stopped, looking back.

"Why did you lie?" she asked.

He spun, kneeling down to meet her eyes. "Those are dangerous men," he whispered. "I'll be honest with you, child; not all men in the tower are good. I don't know what they're about, but you have to promise me you'll never speak of this to anyone."

"I promise," she said quietly, her eyes darting across his mask as she tried to understand.

"Good lad," he said, caressing the back of her head where he'd taught her to tie her hair into a bun under the mask straps. "Now let's get some horses so I can get you safe."

He took her hand, moving her away from the looming maw of the duke's tent. Still, he couldn't help but look over his shoulder to the north. Somewhere out there, Prince Bitan could be dying, and there was nothing he could do to stop it. There was nothing he could do at all.

THE END OF PART TWO

A Respite

Pen'dil Deyn - Time Unknown

—:—

Po'es nol Vireshi, head of the Vindeista and sitting king of the guild council, was *hot*. The sun was already baking the central square, and the walk from the merchant's guild to the sacred tower felt longer than ever. Of course, no one else seemed to mind. To most in Pen'dil Deyn, spring was a blessing. Men and women littered the square in various states of undress, apparently oblivious to the heat as their arms shone in the afternoon light.

"Bloody loungers," he said under his breath. Didn't anyone know there was money to be made? Perhaps he ought to be grateful. As his father always said, the only reason merchants made money was because most people were too foolish to mind their own.

"Sorry, my lord?" his attendants said from behind him where they were holding his court robes off the cobblestones. They were made of sumptuous gold-dyed kelo wool, though they were clearly part of the problem on a day like this.

"Nothing, nothing," Po'es said, waving them off. There was no point in airing his grievances with his servants. The men were too cowed to make good conversation and he couldn't bear their secret judgments besides. He knew the bloody zinc knights called him the Lard King. Bastards.

He wasn't even all that big of a man! He just ate properly like his father had taught him to, and he ate *quality* food — as befit his station. Still, in everyone's rush to worship the zinc lords, they seemed to think every man should have the body of a horse, all muscle and sinew. Had they forgotten they lived in the mountains? He had a blacksmith's body, just like the Snow Father's, and even as a merchant, he knew he could lift both his attendants over his shoulder before they even got to squeaking out their pleasantries.

Part of him longed for the day when the kingship would rotate to the next guild in line. His wife always said he ought to retire, and on days like these, it sounded like a dream. He could see other men of his guild — merchants who were richer than him if not smarter — as they rode about in chairs, carried by their servants. Meanwhile, even with the crown on his head, he was forced to cross the square on foot, all part of some silly sense of propriety passed down from the Snow Father. *"All tools come from the same iron,"* he'd liked to say. But if men were all equal, why had Arikai nol D'ek held the throne until he died?

Unfortunately, it seemed he may be stuck on the throne. There was only one year until the next rotation, but the way the zinc lords were scrambling about the city, they may well have to break the wheel and keep power with the Vindeista for another cycle. The other guilds would probably go for it, of course. No one in their right minds trusted the knights after they destroyed the city — bloody rats! But did he have what it took to remain their king? Five more years of walking in the sun and sitting in a lousy gilded chair? A bloody waste of coin, this kingship was.

They reached the center of the square, the massive pillars of zinc and cobalt glistening in the sun. Po'es stepped up onto the sacred circle of stone, the little shortcut across the square — and a break from the sun in the pillars' shadow — one of the only privileges afforded to him. His attendants let go of his robes, letting the cloth fall to the sacred ground as they scurried around to pick it back up on the other side.

Only on the pedestal did people finally seem to notice his passing. A few nearby merchants stopped their conversation, bowing, and a young boy pulled on his mother's skirt, pointing. Still, the moment he stepped off, the spell was broken. The city moved on, like some great beast letting out a yawn, the cycle never broken for long. Besides, even if the people had cared to look, they had their own guild leaders to look at.

As he stepped through the pillars, the other guild leaders were arriving from their own trips across the square, each one's path guided by their own inscrutable traditions. Their attendants didn't hold their robes, but these men were set apart all the same, crowds parting around them, their heads held high. He supposed that was just as well. The Guild Council was what truly mattered in Deyn. After all, even in his little stint as king, it wasn't like he'd earned extra votes; he just got to call the motions. He was a glorified secretary, a flunky in golden robes — even if the royal suites were the nicest quarters he'd ever seen...

Secretary or not, though, the other council members waited for him at the entrance to the sacred tower, forming a half-circle and bowing as he passed them. He waved them off, eager to get under the shade. He still had a long climb before he reached his throne, and uncomfortable as it was, he found himself longing for it all the same.

Stepping into the torchlight, his eyes adjusting to the dark, he found members of the city guard standing at attention in front of the statue of the Snow Father. Unfortunately, among them was the city garrison chief, Ner'ske Remir'an, bloody zinc dog. While the merchant guilds technically had control of the guard in the city center, the men were still stationed in barracks with the zinc knights, and it was hard to trust any man who served two thrones. Ner'ske, with his bloody mustache, *smiled* as he bowed, as if he knew a joke Po'es didn't. Were those bastards planning something?

He glanced at the statue of the Snow Father as he passed. He almost prayed for protection — some aid from the gods in the troubles clearly brewing — but he held his tongue. The giant statue looked ahead, his eyes only for his precious pillars. The Snow Father didn't care about what happened to the people of this city. If he had, he would have killed the Zinc Father a thousand years ago, stripping the snake Irem nol Chirem's head from his body. The zinc knights were a poison, and one that would surely kill the rest of them if he didn't do something about it.

Po'es began the climb to the throne room, following the steep stone stairs as they spiraled around the outside of the tower. As he reached the second floor, he paused, sucking in a few deep breaths before continuing. Luckily, their obsession with propriety meant the others couldn't start up the stairs until he reached the top of each flight, giving him a moment's rest before continuing the climb. On the other hand, he only needed to rest in the first place because of the Snow Father's obsession with the pillars. The second floor had nothing in it, just a giant set of windows facing the hunks of metal.

Why had Arikai nol D'ek loved those damn pillars so much? He seemed to think they offered some strength to the guild council, but if they had a purpose, he'd never found one. If only they had some weapon to use against the knights… What was the power of the purse compared to a thousand magic swords? He'd been working on restricting metal imports to strangle their forge, but that did nothing to stop the weapons the knights already had from turning on him.

He started up the next staircase, letting out a sigh of relief when he saw the throne room. There were nine thrones in all — and one "chair" for the zinc king who never attended — circled around another one of the Snow Father's little toys, the cobalt altar. Supposedly cut from the forge itself, it glittered in the sunlight from the window, its perfectly smooth surface reflecting the sky above and the pillars below.

Po'es crossed the room, sitting on his throne. But as the others filed in, he couldn't take his eyes off the altar, wishing it had some answer for him. Used for the Snow Father's blood magic, it was the strongest bit of magic they had on this side of the city. But no one used blood magic anymore, did they? Outside of medicine, of course. Perhaps the priests knew of a use for it that could counter the knights. Perhaps—

"The council is in attendance," the tower's chief steward called out as the other council members took their seats.

Po'es sighed, rubbing his forehead. A problem for another day, perhaps.

"Alright," he said, "let's begin."

After all, he had a city to run. He just had to make sure there was something left of it before his reign was up.

———

Pen'dil Seln - Time Unknown
—:—

Theiral sat in the grass looking out at the horizon. He could sense another storm brewing, but it hardly mattered. It wasn't like they would let him back in the tents just because he had a warning to share. Especially after they'd ignored him when he had something truly important to say… He worried for the sheep, of course, but Rikosh had ability enough to warn everyone in time. He simply had to wait here, letting the tides of Flow wash over him until the grass told him the others were leaving.

Some days he felt like a sheep himself, wandering the fields in search of food. The garden mothers left him a basket every morning with something to eat, leaving it covered in grass so the elders wouldn't see. At least someone was still on his side. He pictured Father's face, squeezing his eyes shut — though it did little to block the memory.

"You've shamed me," was all Father had said, turning his back on Theiral. He'd chosen the elders and the tents — and a way of life that no longer made any sense. If only there were someone as powerful as him, someone else who could hear the statue's whispers. But even Rikosh, whose powers were only strong enough to sense storms, had testified before the elders that Theiral was lying.

Perhaps he should have left his people. He could sense even now the other herds in the basin, the power of their Flow coming to him through the grass. But for some reason, he couldn't bring himself to abandon the people who'd betrayed him, not when *something* was coming. He didn't know what, but three months ago, the statue's whispers had grown…*urgent,* as if they'd wanted to warn him.

Of course, it was just one mystery amongst dozens in the Mother's Valley. He'd had plenty of time to ponder those these past few months, banished with nothing to do but wait for the herd to move again. He scooped up a handful of grass, smelling its sweet perfume before he let it drift off in the wind. Take these fields. They said the other basins had only stone, so why did Pen'dil Seln have grass? Was it because they sat closest to the god mount, the life of Sen'el'seng close at hand? Or was it because of Father Serimin, the true worship of Flow giving them access to the grass no one else could grow?

Perhaps he'd never know. Perhaps he'd sit here until he grew old, until the herd—

"Bahhhhh!"

Theiral looked up, seeing a lamb on the rise above him. He cursed, running toward the poor creature. He scooped the lamb up, looking at the tents over the hill.

"Why'd you leave the herd, little one?" he cooed, stroking its head. It happened every now and again, especially with the lambs. It was almost as if they could sense the Flow in him, confusing it for the statue of Father Serimin. He always urged them home eventually, but this time, with a storm coming, there wouldn't be time. He would survive just fine, of course, hiding in whatever nook he could hunt out in the hills. But this lamb was a newborn, its spring coat hardly warm enough to beat the rain.

He glanced at the village again, spotting the first storm cloud to the north. It was almost like they *came* from Sen'el'seng, the god mount churning out dark clouds that would soon cover the valley. Just another mystery, and not one that would help him get this baby home. He shook his head, starting the walk toward the tents. He wouldn't go all the way, of course, but maybe if he got the lamb close enough without being seen, it would go the rest of the way on its own.

Sitosarunal, the pillar whispered. Even here, hundreds of feet away, he could hear it, its sacred voice carrying to him on the currents of Flow coursing through the grass. He pulled back his foot as if burned, clamping his eyes shut as the vision came for him again, the throbbing light in his mind. Why did it sound like a woman? Was it the Sacred Mother speaking through Father Serimin?

He wanted to follow it, *needed* to listen to it, but he couldn't. The voices had already gotten him banished. What would happen now if he really listened to them? The elders barely tolerated him skulking back here like some wolf. If they made him leave for good, there'd be no one to protect his people, no one to find the lost lambs in the endless sea of grass.

"Little one," he said, meeting the lamb's eyes as he set it down. "You need to go back on your own. Please."

The lamb bleated again, nibbling on his fingers. Theiral took a deep breath. Perhaps something to coax him home.

He summoned Flow, feeling the power of the grass around him. Beneath his feet, he could feel its secrets, the way the roots reached into the soil, the water traveling underneath, like another river beneath the stone. There was incredible life in these fields, all of it pulsing toward the statue — and the other carvings of Father Serimin throughout the basin, each one tended to by another set of tents, another set of elders.

He scooped up some of that power in his mind, sending it back toward the statue. He wasn't sure how, but the sheep were able to sense Flow. No one in the village understood that — they simply thought the sheep sought out the best grass to eat, dragging the village with them as they grazed. But it was Flow the sheep were following, the current of life itself.

The lamb bleated one last time, jumping like a little goat. But it seemed to understand, and it chased after the wave of Flow, running in the direction of the village. He watched it go until he heard someone shout from the tents, pointing at the lamb running across the field.

Theiral ducked down, sliding back into the grass. He was nothing more than a ghost in the fields now. But at least he was close enough to watch. A storm was coming, a *real* storm, and he would be there to protect his people when it came.

PART THREE

A Journal

I feel like the Snow Father himself. I've done the unthinkable, making an impossible wealth of metal. This goes beyond the zinc pillars. This is the power of the gods themselves, enough to make Deyn a giant among the kingdoms. But all anyone can talk about is those Zennan ambassadors. Will this really mean war?

-Journal of Serimh nal Akistore:
963ʳᵈ Year of Finding, 3ʳᵈ of Sanimira
16 Years Ago

—:—

20

Serimh scurried about the throne room, finishing his preparations. An audience didn't make for good science — least of all an audience of bloody *fa'ncoli* knights. Still, he knew his business, and after a frantic night without sleep in the workshop, he'd finally perfected the process. It had taken a full liter of homogenous blood — a request the knights had been disgustingly eager to fulfill — but at long last, he was ready.

"Priest," his minder said from the door, "the council grows tired of waiting."

"Nearly there," he said without looking up from the iron plate. "You can send them up."

There was no snide remark at that, the knight leaving to get the council. The knights would never respect him, but they were stepping carefully now. Even they knew how important this was to their king. Unfortunately, it also meant they were watching him more closely than ever. His letters were arriving already opened now. He'd always known they *could* read his mail, but more often than not in the past, it had at least seemed like they didn't bother. Still, he needed a way out, and he'd need to find one even with them looking over his shoulder. There had to be one more letter he could send, one bridge he hadn't yet burned. Unfortunately, whatever he did, the time between finishing the serosine and escaping would be hopelessly brief.

He heard footsteps in the hallway and quickly stepped to the side as the king walked in. Followed by the others, he didn't even look at Serimh as he made his way around the fire to the throne. In fact, he didn't even look at the implements on the floor, as if a half-dozen iron plates were simply another part of the decor. The rest of the council followed after. The king's lessers, at least, seemed interested in his experiment. One of the lords even paused beside one of the plates, peering down at the metal, though a cough from Lord Stal got him moving again. As they took their seats, a pair of knights shut the doors, the ominous groan of the metal filling the room.

"Serimh nal Akistore," Lord Stal said from the king's side. "I trust you're prepared to deliver on what you promised?"

"I think you'll find, my lord," he said, stepping off the wall with his hands behind his back, "that I've exceeded expectations."

The iron plates were arranged in a circle around a serosine box in the center, each plate already prepared with a perfect circle of blood. He lifted the handles on the side of the box, revealing a large block of ice brought down from the mountains. They'd pushed back on his request for the serosine at first — as if he hadn't made it himself! — though at least they complied in the end.

"I began with iron, following in the footsteps of the Snow Father. He needed Passion to light his fires, but it was blood magic that guaranteed the flames never went out."

"Enough," the king said, waving his hand. "We didn't ask for a history lesson, priest."

Serimh put the box back, bowing. There was no love lost between the zinc knights and the Snow Father. They probably wished Irem nol Chirem had founded the basin himself, if only to let their bloodlust run free. No matter. He'd shown them the ice; the rest of the presentation would speak for itself. There were six blood seals on the serosine box — including on the floor — protecting the ice from all sides. It was the same blood sample he'd used on the iron plates, which should prove his point rather well.

"Behold."

He nodded to the knights along the walls, and they stepped forward, lighting the metal plates with torches. Immediately, they became a bonfire, sweat coming to his forehead as the flames exploded from the iron. The men of the council all squinted save for the king, his hand going to his beard as he watched. Thankfully, despite their power, he'd only set up the plates with enough blood to burn for a minute, and soon, they began to die down.

Serimh stepped carefully through the dwindling fires, careful not to singe his robes. He lifted the box, receiving at least two gasps for his trouble as he revealed the block of ice. It was pristine, not a single drop melted from it despite the blazing heat. Even the serosine in his hands was cool to the touch, as if the Passion of the fires had never been.

"Incredible," Lord Stal said, staring at the ice. "You can repeat this with any of the Principles?"

"Yes, my lord," Serimh said. He put the serosine behind him, kicking the block of ice toward one of the dying flames. The ice began to sweat, its surface no longer protected.

"Call the full guild," the king said. "They should know of our intentions. But more importantly, we need that Zennan blood."

The council began talking amongst themselves, seeming to forget Serimh was present as they jockeyed for position. The knights, however, hadn't, and his minder put a hand on his shoulder, steering him from the room.

"Be ready, priest," the knight said, turning him toward the stairs. "It seems you finally have some real work to do."

21

Eyri wandered through the darkness, though she couldn't remember where she was going. She stopped to look around, finding those strange trees overhead again. What had brought her here? What had—

She heard a whisper. She spun in a circle, though she couldn't tell where the voice had come from — or what it had been saying. Suddenly, a waterfall of whispers flooded into her ears. It was how she'd felt in the temple, the voices of the pillars coming to her as she fought to save Borash.

"No," she said, dropping down into a crouch as she covered her ears, squeezing her eyes shut. "You aren't real. Whatever you were, you abandoned me, you—"

She felt a sharp pain in her stomach as a searing heat filled her. It spread into her veins, coursing through her blood and pounding in her temples. She knew that feeling. It was Passion, a power she'd know anywhere, its flame somehow closest to the distorted lives the Masked Ones led. As she focused on it, the whispers fell away. She reached for it, seizing its power, enough to burn the entire forest if she wanted.

She stood, ready to consume the air in flame, when she paused. The forest, completely dark just a moment earlier, was now lit with a blue haze. Ahead of her, on the horizon, a giant star sparkled in the night sky. It was alone, but it was as bright as the moon, the air seeming to *bend* around it. As she stared at it, the whispers began again, only this time, she could almost make out what they were saying. They—

Kouselumakash, a voice whispered, a woman. But it sounded like it came from the star, like it *was* the star.

She ran toward it, but as she left her clearing, pushing through the undergrowth of the forest, the light was blotted out. She stumbled, falling to the ground as time seemed to fall away, until she heard a single word from the star above.

Eyri—

She woke to the sound of a dry cough. She opened her eyes in the darkness, forgetting who she was, *when* she was. She looked for Viden. Was he watching over her again after the war, when they thought the duke might come for them? Was she in the tower? She reached for her sword, but her hand hit something soft beside her. Something small and coughing.

"Teros?" she asked, sitting up in the dark cave, suddenly remembering where she was.

Teros only groaned, letting out another cough. As her eyes adjusted, she could just make out the blue light of dawn outside the cave. Teros was usually up by then, cooking breakfast over the fire. She put a hand to his forehead, finding it hotter than a coal, his brow slick with sweat.

She was immediately on her feet, kicking free of the blankets though she had no idea what to do. Masked Ones never got sick once they ascended. Your first year in the tower, the priests were constantly holding you in the sick bay, blowing powders up your nose and poking tinctures into your back. At first, you got so sick you thought you'd die, but then you were never ill again. You could even go in the chiroptary with no problem, the bat farmers hacking and wheezing until they collapsed.

"You should have let him ascend," a voice said in her mind.

A horrible thought. As if she could have let him suffer that. She'd seen him in the temple, the little mask in Keroes nir Sen'l's hands. She'd drawn her sword to save him, hadn't she? Or had that been for Borash? She'd been willing to sacrifice Teros before that, letting him swear the stone. But what now? She was all he had, his mother and sister in one. And Teros was all *she* had too. But how was she meant to protect him? How was she meant to keep the world from tarnishing this brilliant boy? He couldn't fight. He got ill. He was soft. He—

Teros let out another groan, rolling over, his forehead glistening in the dim light. Her hands formed into fists, going to her temples as she closed her eyes. *Stop thinking and act.* She dropped to her knees beside him, running a hand through his hair.

"Teros. Wake up, okay?"

He cracked his eyes open.

"Eyri?" he asked. "Everything hurts."

"I know," she said, cupping his face. "You're sick. Have you ever felt like this before?"

"Once," he whispered, closing his eyes again.

"What…did your mother do?"

"Soup," he said. "And medicine."

"What kind?"

He shook his head, his eyes still closed.

She got up, going to what was left of their fire as she added some logs to the embers. She'd have to get some porridge going at least. She remembered the priests putting rags on her forehead. She took their 'kitchen towel,' a rag they'd torn from an old grain bag, dipping it in their water bucket. She jogged back to Teros, putting it on his forehead.

"I'll go into town, okay? We need medicine."

What they really needed was someone who knew what they were doing, but she left that part out. Her neck hot with shame, she hurried from the cave, her hands shaking as she took apart the moss covering their little cavern. As afraid as she was, the voice in her mind was worse. She was no mother to him. A mother would have known what to do.

She came down the hill at a jog, only keeping herself from sprinting because she knew she'd need the strength to get back up the mountain. As she came across the valley, she could see smoke rising from the chimneys in Hv'rano. But it was the free day — and still terribly early besides. Would anyone be down in the village? Was she meant to knock on doors until someone helped her? She knew the way people looked at her in town. Like Teros had said all those weeks ago, these people thought they were ghosts. Except Teros had *joined* them, making himself real while she was left screeching in the mountains, her soul lost forever.

When she'd first heard the Deynen legends during the war, she'd thought they were ridiculous. Losing your mind without a guild to tell you what your purpose was? After all, these were the people who thought them demons just for wielding more than one principle. More importantly, *everyone* already had a purpose, didn't they? She'd known hers from five years old, giving everything to serve her family and the crown.

But now? She spared a glance for the mountains as she ran, their peaks disappearing in the morning mist. She'd lost all the things gluing her together. She would do it all over again, of course. There had been a toll to pay and she'd paid it, securing Teros's freedom. But now they were at a door she couldn't open. Teros was drifting away, becoming realer, while she was still a ghost, desperate to right the wrongs the world had forced upon her. But now that he was sick, she was forced to face just how powerless she really was.

She almost felt a tear come to her eye, but she ran faster instead, growling as she burst into the village. By some miracle, she found a woman coming out of the guild house. Her shawl was up over her white hair, a guild symbol stitched on the side by her ears. A village elder, maybe? The woman's eyes widened as she noticed Eyri, but she just as quickly looked behind her at the path into the mountains, no doubt wondering where Teros was.

Eyri stopped, her lungs heaving as she scoured her mind for the words in Deynen. But she'd only been at war with these people. She knew how to say dead — gods forbid it ever came to that! — but she had no idea how to say sick.

"Teros anndar," she panted. *Bad,* the only word she could think of.

"Sva'syg?" the woman asked, putting a hand to her chest as she pantomimed a cough.

Sva'syg," Eyri said, nodding. "Medicine," she said desperately in her own tongue, motioning like she was drinking something down.

"Baribhna me'ghtan sva'syg tashtara arb'voro," the woman said, swinging the door to the guild house back open as she stepped back inside.

The meeting tables had been pushed to the side, a dozen sleeping mats rolled out on the ground. A bunch of children were there, their foreheads glistening like Teros's in the glow of a blazing fire. She felt a spike of anger, realizing Teros had gotten sick at his school, but it wasn't like she could keep him well forever. More importantly, she didn't dare offend this woman lest she deny them what they needed.

Stepping back out, the woman handed Eyri a dark brown bottle. It had some kind of liquid inside, coating the sides of the glass as it sloshed about.

"Lae'del," the woman said. *"Do drabf hvur ogni."* She motioned as if she were taking off the cap as she held up two fingers.

Eyri knew the word for hour. So two drops every hour? She nodded. *"Siul'sho,"* she said, reaching for the coins she kept hidden in her robes.

The woman shook her head, smiling. *"Lif Teros."*

Eyri looked down at the medicine, staring at it in her hand. That was certainly something she couldn't have done for Teros. Maybe he *was* in good hands here. If only she could be sure that was enough in this world...

"Dey'n'lof," she said, thanking the woman as she walked away in a daze.

She drifted toward the village gates, finally remembering herself as she started up the hill at a jog. She needed to get Teros this medicine as quickly as possible. She didn't want to risk another second of leaving him on his own, coughing in a wet cave. But she also needed him well so she could return to her work, so she could be useful to Teros in the only way she knew how.

22

22nd of Selomira 979
Rule of the Vindeista
(24th of Perat-kam, 985, 23rd Year of Iron)

Chir sat on his veranda, sipping his tea as he stared down at the forge. On the slope of the hill to the central city, he'd bought the house when his business first started picking up. It had felt like a throne then, soaring above the Zinc Quarter. It had been almost too luxurious for him — a man who'd started life as a page boy for the army — but he'd bought it for Sonote. This was a house that could last generations. It wouldn't be enough for a king, obviously, but it would have been perfect for a knight rising through the Zamaks. It even had running water from the falls and room for a half-dozen servants.

Now, it was a prison, its walls built of everything they'd taken from him. Even if he only had one day off a week, he could *feel* this place looming over him at the smithy, waiting to swallow him back up. Every night, as he walked up the hill, its lights leered at him, reminding him that his daughter-in-law waited for him above. They were like two mountains of grief, separated by his guilt and stripped of any comfort by the growing gap between them. It felt sometimes like they'd lost two completely different children, their sorrow of entirely different shades.

Take this morning. He still forced himself to take his bitter tea on the veranda, sipping it slowly so he could stare at the forge and remind himself of what he'd done. He even took it without honey now — that little bit of sweetness more than he deserved — drinking down the entire pot of mountain herbs until his stomach turned. Meanwhile, his daughter-in-law was drowning in desserts. She made a feast each day of all the things Sonote had loved, eating as much as she could before giving the rest to the neighbors.

He could hear her banging around in the kitchen, the sharp tang of moss smoke filling the air. He didn't begrudge her whatever sweetness she could find, of course. He'd learned early on in the army how different grief could look depending on who it struck. One knight might ride off in bloodlust while another never took up his blade again. Unfortunately, it was just another thing keeping them apart. But why shouldn't they grieve differently? After all, she wasn't the one who'd killed Sonote.

He heard her footsteps approaching, and he sighed, turning to face her. She still checked on him every hour, refilling his hot water with such deference you'd never know he'd ruined her life. As she stepped through the door, though, her eyes were wide, no water pot in her hand.

"There's a knight waiting for you in the garden."

"A knight?" he asked, frowning. "Why?"

"He didn't say." She glanced toward the front of the house. "He only said you were to come right away."

Was this the end? Had Iremi nal Miri finally decided to kill off all who still opposed him?

"If I don't come back by noon, go to your sister's and don't come back."

He walked slowly through the house, realizing he wasn't afraid. He'd tried to change Deyn and failed. Now he was just…tired. Finished. What did it matter if they killed him?

He put on his cloak and opened the door, but as he laid eyes on the knight, his blood boiled again. It seemed there was still something he hated more than himself. If only he could kill them all! But wasn't that the problem all along? He had no power. He was an old man, and the only strength he'd had was burnt up on Sonote's pyre. The king had shown him what true power was. It wasn't a blade; it was changing the rules as you saw fit.

"What is it?" Chir asked from the porch, his hand still on the door.

The knight hadn't left his horse, but he had another beside him, both sets of reins in his hands.

"Emergency guild meeting," the knight said. "Your presence is requested."

He nodded to the other horse, though he made no moves to help Chir into the saddle.

"Very well," Chir said, climbing up with as much dignity as he could. It had been a decade at least since he'd ridden, but like all zinc steeds, it was a war horse, and it knew to follow its knight without bucking its rider. Perhaps it wasn't the most respectful way of summoning him, but if they *were* going to kill him, it was an odd way of doing it.

As they reached the little tower, they entered a sea of other men just like him, a battalion of guild members on horses escorted by knights. He kept his eyes glued to the tower as they entered the courtyard, unable to stomach looking back at the arena. Even as he forced himself to stare at the forge each day, he couldn't bear to look east, to where Sonote died. *Coward,* he thought, cursing himself. You'd think after killing his own grandson, he'd at least have enough backbone to look.

When they finally stopped, all the knights clambered off their horses, hurrying to help the guild members down. But not his. His knight stayed in his saddle.

"Blacksmith," he said, nodding toward the tower steps.

So it wasn't his life the council wanted, but his spirit. They wanted him to soak in the shame of his failure. What pleasure would there be in killing him when they could make him suffer for another fifteen years? This was to be his punishment. For killing Lord Stal's son, for *daring* to threaten the way of things, they wanted to make a *spo'gimes* of him, a shell with no purpose cursed to wander the earth.

He certainly deserved to be cursed, but he refused to break for these men. Even if he was destroyed on the inside, he would never bow. Sonote deserved more than that. He straightened his back, picking his head up as he joined the crowd moving into the tower. Let them see how strong he could be. For Sonote's legacy, let them see.

The guild hall was the first room off the grand entryway, the council room and its throne hidden above. Like the arena in miniature, the guild hall had the same cursed rows of seats, forcing everyone to sit in the same assignments. Although, perhaps that was the point. If you kept your seat — and your tongue — out there, you got to keep it in here, and all the power that came with it. The seats wrapped around a dais in the center for the king, and Iremi nal Miri was already there with all his lords, surrounded by guards as the guild members filed in.

He sat without speaking to any of his neighbors, but it was just as well. The moment the last person was through the doors, there were knights already there to slam them, the crown squire calling the meeting to order.

"We bring you here," the king said the moment it was quiet, "to discuss a topic of great importance."

"As many of you know," Lord Stal said, standing, "the war did little to dissuade the bloodthirsty nature of our cousins in the west. We've long thought peace would not hold, and it seems we were right. Our sources in Zenn tell us they prepare for war again, but this time, they mean to conquer this basin for good."

The room burst into a storm of heated whispers. It was rubbish, of course. There wouldn't have been a war if Deyn hadn't dammed the river, and the Zennans had no reason to try to conquer them. Deyn had the forge, true, but Zenn already had everything they could ever want, with plenty of food and warm enough weather to have no need for cobalt spikes. Still, it was no surprise the council would eventually stir talk of war. They hated how much power they'd lost in the basin, and another conflict would be the best way to get it back. This was precisely why he and Sonote had fought, what the lad had *died* fighting.

"It is for this purpose we've made fresh serosine," the king said, silencing the whispers — even as what he said deserved a thousand curses. All Chir could picture was the metal bracers at the duel, the glowing arms they'd used to kill Sonote. "We aim to win this war and stomach the things our predecessors couldn't."

The king waved a hand, and a man in priests' robes stepped up, setting up a ring of iron plates around a box. The box had the shimmery glow of serosine, but what would he—

The man grabbed a torch from a knight, setting fire to the iron plates. The flames glowed off the king's eyes, leaping above the dais. Just as quickly, they were out, and the priest was removing the box to reveal a perfect block of ice, untouched by the fire. More whispers broke out at that, but the king was already speaking again, yelling above the din.

"We mean to go further than our ancestors, combining the power of our serosine with the ancient strength of blood magic. We will turn their masked demons into nothing more than children, their necks like grain to be harvested by our swords."

The crowd erupted in cheers at that. *Bloody fools.* Had they forgotten their own children dying on the western flats? Or did they perhaps simply want to profit, uncaring who died for them to make their coin? Blood magic or not, it would only mean death. The masked demons could not be defeated. They'd proven that much during the war a hundred times over.

"We require," Lord Stal said slowly, regaining control of the room, "your assistance and discretion. To make the serosine as powerful as it can be, we need the blood of a Zennan. But we can't just pluck any stray from the street. We don't need to tell you that the Vindeista look to own this city. If the merchant's guild were to hear of us hunting their business partners, they could break the wheel, stripping us of what little power we have left."

"You will find us a worthy candidate," the king said, their plans clearly no longer a request. "Select a Zennan who will not be missed, who you know to be a safe choice for our purpose."

Chir immediately thought of Eyri. The girl was a wonder with the forge, but she had no one save her son. Of course, he'd never give the girl over to them. He liked her, and besides, why would he ever give the bastards the satisfaction? Why would he—

"The person who succeeds in this," Lord Stal continued, "will be granted the title of First Quartermaster."

First Quartermaster… That would give him control of the armory along with all their precious serosine. He never could have imagined rising so high during the war, but that would shove the king right into his hands.

No. He couldn't do that, could he? Eyri had a son… But what of Sonote? He'd already given up his own grandson for the cause. If he was willing to do that, but not this, what did that mean for every other sacrifice he'd made along the way? What of his vengeance? He could barely look his daughter-in-law in the eye as it was. Could he go on living knowing he'd passed up an opportunity to put a blade in the zinc king's heart?

"That is all," Lord Stal said, dismissing the crowd. "If you have a candidate, send for a knight immediately."

Conversations started on every side, men tripping over themselves to get out into the city and seek their reward. But Chir didn't move. His mind whirred, tearing itself in half as he struggled with his choice. He let the others flood around him, staring at the tiny box of serosine on the dais as he wished he'd have the strength for what came next.

23

22ⁿᵈ of Selomira 979
Rule of the Vindeista
(24ᵗʰ of Perat-kam, 985, 23ʳᵈ Year of Iron)

Serimh stayed in the voting hall until only the Zinc Lords remained. They began talking amongst themselves, clearly forgetting he was present at all. Still, he lingered. With the lords chasing after their own plans like rabbits in the mountains, he felt the trap closing around his neck. Even as he performed *miracles* with their serosine, he was no closer to his freedom. This was his final chance to gain some control over his life, his last opening for leverage. An idea had come to him in the night, one he felt he had to try. But would they see through it?

"My lords," he said, the whispering ceasing as a dozen pairs of cold eyes turned on him. He swallowed, finally noticing the knights by the door with their hands on their swords. Still, he wouldn't get a chance like this again.

"I believe we need to discuss the...*parameters* of this experiment. It was easy enough to bond a little circle of blood with iron, but what you propose is far more difficult. Bonding liters of fresh blood — with unknown blends of Zennan principles, mind you — requires equipment I simply do not have."

"We've already told you we'll supply you with anything you need, priest," Lord Longfan said. "Do not waste the council's time with issues you should have taken up with your keepers."

"I apologize for not speaking more clearly, my lord," Serimh said, bowing quickly. "The thing I need is not so easily acquired. It is...delicate, just as it is vital."

"Out with it then."

"The amount of bonding required, with the volatile components I've been given... Well, my lord, the only person capable of such feats was the Snow Father. If I am to succeed, I'll need access to his altar."

He was met with silence again. Only this time, it was *heavier* somehow, the impact of what he'd said landing in the council like the fireball of a masked demon. But in a way, it *was* true. He needed more power, more *magic* to see this through. It may be terribly convenient that the thing he needed was in the city center, potentially returning him to his own study — and what might be his last chance to gather what money he could and escape. The question was whether or not this council of bloodthirsty lordlings would see that.

As quickly as they'd fallen into their stunned silence, the lords seemed to remember themselves, snippets of their frantic whispering reaching his ears.

"—little control over the guard as it is, we—"

"There is *some* flexibility with the payroll—"

"—if the altar were—"

"If we move too early, and the Vindeista—"

"Enough," the king said, silencing them as he raised a hand. He leaned forward, staring into Serimh's eyes. "You've made your disdain for this work clear enough, priest. How do we know this isn't a scheme to reveal our hand to the money-grubbers? You think the merchant guild would just hand us the keys to the central tower while Po'es nol Vireshi sits on the throne?"

It was one thing to face Lord Longfan, sticking your head into the bear's cave. It was quite another to have the zinc king stare at you. Suddenly, his mouth felt drier than the western flats, his pulse pounding in his temples.

"The holiday," he managed to get out, the final piece of his plan to convince them. "Baker's Day. The entire city will be at the parade. If we can sneak into the sacred tower, I can do in a single hour what would take me months here."

Iremi nal Miri flicked his eyes over to Lord Longfan, an eyebrow raised.

"The central tower is held by the city guard," Longfan said, "but they do report to our garrison chief. I've seen a list before of...*reliable* individuals, soldiers more suited to the old ways. Perhaps if we can adjust the shifts..."

The king nodded to himself, his cold grey eyes turning on Serimh again.

"I give you one last chance. What you say is true? This is absolutely needed for my serosine?"

Somehow, Serimh kept himself from swallowing the lump in his throat. It wasn't lost on him that the zinc lords kept calling it the 'central' tower. To them, there was nothing sacred about the Snow Father. Still, he knew, too, that blood magic was the one thing they felt was beyond their power. They may hold the swords of memory, but they only cared for Identity, the power of the wind. *This* was his chance.

"The Zinc Father was a powerful man," he said carefully. "Perhaps the most powerful we've ever seen. After all, the Snow Father had no knights of his own. But the Snow Father *did* know blood magic, my lord. I promise you this is essential. Give me access to the tower, and I'll shower you in serosine."

The king made a fist, knocking his throne. His chief minder, the most loathsome of the knights, rushed over from the door, going to one knee as he bowed his head.

"You will speak with the garrison chief," the king said. "Prepare to give the priest what he needs."

"My lord," the knight said, standing.

"But—" the king added, looking at Serimh. "If he gives you even a hint of betrayal, kill him."

24

By the time morning came around, Teros was just…better. He was up at the fire, making breakfast as he hummed to himself. Eyri came out of the cave, rubbing her eyes as she joined him.

"You seem well again," she said, watching him stir the gruel. Was this just how children were? She hadn't had a childhood, but she certainly didn't remember people being so hardy. She couldn't really recall any of her neighbors from Mer'n Hill, but she had the odd feeling her parents had dragged her to plenty of funerals.

"Fine now," Teros said, smiling. "Sorry I worried you. Was…the medicine expensive?"

"It was free," she said, chuckling as she took the bowl he offered her. "It seems you really do have friends down in the village."

"Oh," he said, looking in the direction of Hv'rano as if he could see it through the mountain. "Do you know who gave it to you? I'll have to thank them."

She suddenly felt a stab of…what, jealousy? She pictured the woman's face from the village, her chest suddenly hot at the thought of Teros thanking her. Would she hug him? Pat him on the head? She was the one who taught Teros every day, making him one of her own boys in a way. And maybe it was a good thing in a larger sense. After all, it proved Teros had *some* way of protecting himself. His friends in the village were something he'd made for himself, but it was something she had no access to, a world she could never reach.

"I'm not sure," she said, swallowing. "She was older, with guild stitches on her shawl."

He nodded. "I think that's my teacher."

Eyri forcefully shoveled gruel into her mouth, barely tasting it as she swallowed. She felt guilt bubbling up beside her jealousy, but she couldn't seem to snuff out either. It was an ugly feeling, a petty feeling. And—

Teros came around the fire, standing before her. She looked up as he gave her a full bow.

"I'm sorry I made you worry," he said. "Thank you for getting the medicine."

She stared at him, bowl in hand until she realized he was staying bowed, his eyes locked on the ground.

"It's…it's okay," she said, putting her bowl down as she opened her arms. "Come here, you have nothing to apologize for."

He hugged her, her fingers dancing through his hair. Somehow, the dark feelings slipped away. Why couldn't she feel this way all the time? In moments like these, she felt like an actual mother. Or what she imagined a mother to be like, anyway… Perhaps real mothers fought with their children too. But with so little time between them, so few months of being free, it all left her feeling lost.

She finally let him go, standing so she could put her cloak on. "I've got to head to work. Why don't you go lay down? You didn't have to cook today, you know."

"Actually…" he said slowly, looking up from where he'd went back to fiddling with the porridge. "I wanted to go to town today. We're picking grass for Baker's Day."

She'd forgotten all about the holiday, of course. Presumably they were already decorating in the city, but the zinc knights didn't seem to care for such frivolities — and she couldn't blame them. Weren't there more important things than festivals? Even if the zinc knights were her enemies, it seemed soldiers would always have more in common than regular folk.

"Do you really think you should be out picking flowers in your condition?"

Of course, she kept her opinions on the holiday to herself. She could already imagine the sad look that would wash over his face, and for some reason, she couldn't bring herself to do that to him. Maybe holidays weren't for soldiers, but Teros *wasn't* one. In fact, he was nothing like her — more often than not in wonderful, beautiful ways. And perhaps he'd never be.

"I feel fine," he said, "and I'm sure everyone else is too. Please let me go. I promise I'll come home if I get tired. It's just my first holiday here — well, my first real one, anyway — and I don't want to miss anything this time."

His first *real* holiday. She thought of the Day of Joy and the fireworks she'd barely let him see, the holiday shrunk to nothing more than a glare against the mountain.

"Alright," she said, sighing. "But if you get any sicker, I'm not letting you go to that parade."

"Of course," he said, nodding quickly as he covered up the breakfast pot. "You won't regret it."

He ran back to the cave, grabbing his school things as if afraid she'd change her mind. Maybe this *was* mothering, especially with a child as gifted as Teros. After all, he was learning and he was happy. Of course, it would only make it harder when they finally left Pen'dil Deyn, but she wouldn't deny him his tiny pleasures, especially the ones *she'd* never had. Soldier or not, she had to do right by him. How else could she live with herself?

She chuckled, grabbing her own things as he ran off.

"Don't push yourself!" she called after him, but he was already gone, off into that world she knew next to nothing about.

25

23ʳᵈ of Selomira 979
Rule of the Vindeista
(25ᵗʰ of Perat-kam, 985, 23ʳᵈ Year of Iron)

As Teros came down the hill into Hv'rano, the village emerging from the mist like a river pearl, the place was busier than usual. The farmers were always up early, of course, wandering about the fields with their tools, but it seemed like the whole village was in the square. Was this all for the grass cutting?

He reached the gates, but even as he passed the massive cobalt spikes, the place was already transformed. Woven baskets lined the street, what seemed like hundreds of them of every conceivable shape and size. Woven out of grass like something from Pen'dil Seln, there was even one shaped like a hawk, the sides formed into giant wings. Others had dried flowers woven into the sides, splashing the patterns with bursts of color.

As he reached the guild house, he found his teacher outside, adding baskets to the display. These ones were simpler, rounded things, though their construction was still elegant. It seemed impossible that something as flimsy as grass could become something so ornate. His teacher noticed him, smiling, and he finally remembered himself, bowing low to the ground.

"Thank you for the medicine. I'm sorry I got sick."

"You're your mother's child, alright," she said, laughing as she gently put a hand on his shoulder to pull him back to standing. "Apologizing for being sick is like wishing it wasn't raining."

His mother's child… He suddenly realized what it must have taken for Eyri to come here and ask for help. He felt his neck burn with shame, though it was an oddly comforting compliment too. Was he really like her? He hoped he was, even if he feared he'd never have her strength.

"Is everyone else okay?" he asked, looking around the square. It seemed all of the other children were there, standing in groups with their mothers, their fathers on their way back from the fields.

"Of course," his teacher said. "Have you never had the *Hos't'hovn?*"

He didn't know the word, of course, but it was probably the name of the illness. He shook his head.

"Well, I suppose you're in luck. Hurts something awful, but it's never more than a day — assuming you take your medicine, of course. Anyway, why don't you go find Liska? We're about to begin, and she has tools for you."

He scanned the crowd of villagers again, finally spotting Liska with her brother and mother. She looked…*beautiful,* her hair curling around her head in braids, woven through with ribbons. It reminded him of Mother, the way she'd dress for the end of Sund-z'ar, already like an angel well before she died. Was this what Liska looked like on a holiday?

He almost started whispering to himself, but something held him back. He felt…*nervous,* his feet stuck to the cobblestones. Maybe that was a sign he was doing Mother proud. Being in this place, making friends in Hv'rano. If he was living out his oaths, then there was no need to whisper them, right? Before he could decide what to do, Liska looked up, meeting his eyes. She smiled, waving him over. He took a deep breath, marching across the square.

"Teros, you remember my Mehm?" Liska said, motioning toward her.

"Ma'am," Teros said with a quarter bow. Liska's mother was just as pretty, but they looked different, Liska's nose less hooked and more…*Zennan* somehow? Maybe Liska took after her father? Si'tar, on the other hand, was the spitting image of his mother. Was that what made him a "fireplace boy?"

"Everyone always says you have good manners," Liska's Mehm said, chuckling. "It's good you know how to pick 'em, Lis."

What had Liska picked him for? Teros cocked his head, thinking he'd misunderstood the Deynen. Liska just shot her mother a glare, turning to a cloth-wrapped bundle on the ground between them.

"You can cut grass with us," she said, opening the bundle to reveal four hand sickles. They were like the ones the workers had used on Uncle Elin's farm, only they had metal handles instead of wood, their blades the dark steel of the Deynen forges. Liska picked one up, handing it to him with the blade turned away. He took it, staring down at his reflection in the steel.

"Thank you. I've…never cut grass before. Where is it?"

He looked around the village, eyeing the fields, but the crops had only just begun to sprout under the warmth of the cobalt spikes. Instead, Liska pointed behind him at the hills ringing the town. His eyes widened, finding them covered in grass. When had that popped up? It was a dull green, but it looked like a river of emeralds compared to the black stone of the mountains beyond. It really *was* like Pen'dil Seln, where they said the grass spread like the infinite oceans of the Giant Lands. But how had they made so much soil?

"Dirt is the true wealth, boy," Uncle Elin's voice suddenly said in his mind. Uncle Elin had a ring of grass around his pond, too, something he claimed had taken his workers generations, breaking down the rocks with hammers until it could hold the crops that had made his uncle rich.

"Incredible," he whispered, earning a laugh from Liska.

"See?" she said, turning back to her mother. "He really is a *spo'gimes,* like he's never seen the world before."

Part of him felt he ought to smart at the comparison, but coming from Liska, even being a ghost felt like a compliment. He turned to say as much when a sharp banging sound came from behind him. The village elders had entered the square, his teacher hitting a spoon against a metal pot.

"Alright, everyone!" one of the men called. "It's time to begin the grass cutting. Keep your heart on that special someone and no shoving anyone down the hill this year!"

The villagers swarmed toward the hill, the young ones running ahead of their parents. Liska took him by the elbow, pulling him forward at a trot.

"Why are we running?"

"Everyone wants the good grass!" she said, laughing.

"What's a 'special someone?'" he asked, his breathing picking up as they ran. *Nog'im'saer* was the word the elder had used, literally 'someone precious,' the word *saer* from *saer'd,* the word for jewel. He'd thought he was starting to understand Deynen, but already this morning he felt like he'd only just arrived.

Liska didn't turn around, though she let go of his arm.

"We make the baskets for someone else to use on Baker's Day. Mehms for their children, Peppins for their wives, and the younger ones for someone they like the best. Before we get married in Hv'rano, we always make a basket for that 'special someone.'"

He thought of the baskets lining the path into the village, how intricate the designs had been.

"Those were all made for someone else?"

"Every last one," she said, finally turning and flashing him a smile. "Did you see the dragon? That's the one my Peppin made when he proposed to Mehm."

They reached the hillside, the grass somehow holding onto the steep incline. Villagers started to climb, edging up sideways as they fanned out through the grass.

"Come on," Liska said, pointing at a patch halfway up where the grass was dotted with yellow flowers. "I want flowers in mine, and those patches always go first."

Teros followed her to the spot, mimicking her as she started using her hand sickle to take down big clumps of grass. They laid them down in a pile at their feet, pressing them into the hillside so they wouldn't roll down behind them.

"So?" Liska asked, meeting his eyes before looking away again. "Who'll you make yours for?"

"I'm...not sure," Teros said, standing as he paused. He looked back down at the village, where the line of baskets below had blurred into a single brown mass. "I'm not sure I even know how."

"I'll show you the basic weaves when we're done. You'll have to do the proper parts at home, though — baskets are secret, after all. Just decide who to make it for, and I'll take care of the rest."

Liska was acting strange... Did that mean she wanted him to make her a basket? She *was* his only real friend here, but did that make her his "special someone?" Or…did that mean something else? He gulped, suddenly all too aware of the pretty ribbons in her hair, her braids swaying in the sunlight. Shouldn't he make one for Eyri, though? She never got to experience anything in the village, but she ought to see this. Maybe it would change her mind about Hv'rano. The people were so alive here, so…*happy.* Shouldn't they be happy?

"I wish my mother was here," he said.

Liska paused with her hand on a clump of grass, glancing at him.

"Do you…want to make her a basket?"

"Maybe I should," Teros said. "Or…for you? Can I do both? How much grass do I need?"

"Loads," she said, her smile wide as she cut another huge clump and dumped it on his pile. "But I'll help you."

They worked a while longer, until their piles reached almost to their knees. Other villagers were already heading back down the hill, bundles on their shoulders. Some sat right where they were, though, pulling rolls from their pockets to stop and eat. Liska did the same, pulling a huge slice of bread from her dress.

"Why didn't your Mehm come?" she asked, handing him half the bread. "Does she not know about the holidays either?"

"She had to work," he said, taking a bite of the bread. Like everything in Hv'rano, it was delicious, the wheat flour from their mills almost nutty, the crust cracking with a perfect crunch. All Eyri did was work. At first, he'd felt guilty, of course, useless as he stayed back in the cave while she provided for him. But it seemed the more money they had for food, the harder she worked. Of course, now, more than anything, she wanted the serosine. But what would finding it do? Assuming she didn't get herself killed — the thought of which drowned him in the urge to whisper his lucky words — nothing could undo what happened at the temple, no matter how badly she wished it so.

"I wish she could taste this bread, see this place. She doesn't understand what's *good* about Deyn. She's…looking for something, and she only cares about finding it."

"Her gems?" Liska asked, looking in the direction of the mountains.

He'd almost forgotten that first lie he told. In some ways, though, serosine *was* Eyri's gemstone, her sacred "pearl of the sea" as the Wise Father called it. How could he explain? He thought of his book on Deynen. He'd recently learned the word 'obsessed' — *laug'dvang.* But like everything in Deyn, it was related to something else, like *laugda,* the word for guild, everything wrapped up in their search for a calling.

"She has an…obsession," he said carefully. "And if she doesn't find it, I'm afraid she'll never find peace."

Liska hummed, nodding as she ate her bread, looking off into the distance across the barren stretch of the western flats.

"I think it's good to have something you care about. After all, that's the only difference between us and the *spo'gimes,* isn't it? Sometimes, it just means your obsession and hers aren't the same. That's why people change guilds."

"Maybe you're right," he said. He didn't want to think of 'leaving his guild,' of going to a place Eyri couldn't follow. *Together,* he whispered in his mind. But that also didn't feel quite right, either. They'd had purpose in Zenn — that's *all* they'd had — but a purpose like that burned you up like firewood, erasing everything that made you human. There had to be something more to life — like bread in the sunshine on a hill full of flowers. There had to be something good that wasn't just the end of a sword.

"I get why it's important to pick a guild, to…find somewhere you belong, but there has to be some difference, too, you know? Somewhere where your obsession ends and you begin. Something that's just…*you.*"

Liska laughed, nudging him with another piece of bread.

"You're an interesting one, Teros nir Zi'yun. Zennan to the bone, but interesting as a frozen yak."

He didn't get that reference, but it seemed like a compliment from the way she smiled. And it was a gorgeous smile. Life *was* good here, he just had to help Eyri see that.

26

23ʳᵈ of Selomira 979
Rule of the Vindeista
(25ᵗʰ of Perat-kam, 985, 23ʳᵈ Year of Iron)

Eyri leaned over a hot metal bar, inspecting her work so far. Chir had begun letting her practice shaping the metal herself, but her work was inconsistent. He created perfect bars with barely any blows, no movement wasted as he brought down the hammer in the exact same way every time. That was only one step in dozens to make a sword, of course, but she'd have little hope of learning proper smithing if she couldn't at least do the basics. She'd thought she was learning quickly after perfecting the temperature of the forge and the blend of the metals, but unfortunately, the smithing itself was proving much more difficult than fixing a few chips on her own blade.

She looked up, finding him watching her from his stool. When their eyes met, though, he looked away, glancing out the window. Eyri frowned, pausing for a moment before she took the hammer up again. She'd been afraid he was about to criticize her, but he almost seemed to…*regret* watching her. But what did he have to be ashamed of? It was his forge, his metal. She was the one doing a terrible job of shaping it.

"I wonder," Chir said quietly, her arm freezing with the hammer mid-air, "if you might want to make some extra money?"

She glanced at her bar for a moment, its surface rapidly cooling under her useless dithering. She grabbed it with the tongs, putting it back in the forge to try again.

"How do you mean?" she asked, turning with her arms behind her back. It was hard not to stand at attention when he addressed her, just another clue she had to hide that she was no normal mother.

"Well," he said, rubbing his hands together. "I've been entrusted with a…special shipment by the zinc council. I need to get it to another basin. I won't be able to join the shipment myself with the forge to look after, but… Well, I thought it might be good to have someone I trust aboard, someone who knows their way around a blade. It's just…"

Eyri felt a sudden flush of heat far greater than the forge behind her. The hair on her arms stood up, every part of her prickling with excitement. This had to be the serosine. But would he see her excitement? Would it give her away? She licked her lips, her tongue suddenly drier than the Stone Forest. Chir took a deep breath, his throat bobbing as he swallowed.

"With your son, I wanted to see if he had somewhere he could stay while you're gone. I…wouldn't want to take you if it would leave him hard up."

Of course. She felt the familiar spike of shame climbing up her throat. A real mother wouldn't have to be reminded of her child… But Teros would be fine, wouldn't he? She was always going to have to take a risk to get the serosine. If anything, Teros was in a better place now than he'd ever been. If she somehow failed and didn't come back, he'd be no worse off than he was now. But this was her only chance to get them home, to make something more of their lives than hiding in caves and lurking around the farm folk.

"I can find someone to watch him," she said, trying to speak in a level voice. She couldn't let on what she knew, how excited she was. "When…does this shipment leave?"

"Tomorrow," he said, crossing toward the forge. "I'm sorry you won't get to celebrate Baker's Day with your son, but I wasn't given much notice. In fact, you should take off early today. Celebrate tonight if you can."

He pulled some money from his apron, pushing it into her hand. It was at least triple her normal wage. He took her tongs from the table, going to work on the metal bar.

"I… Are you sure? This is so much money."

"It's nothing," he said, though he didn't meet her eyes. He began working the metal, focused only on his smooth, even strikes. Perhaps he was no fan of the serosine either? It wasn't as though the Deynens hadn't lost things in the war, and with Sonote…

"Thank you," she said. "I won't let you down."

Of course, she *would* let him down. She'd burn every ounce of serosine she could find. But hopefully, by going in his place, she'd spare him. She hadn't expected so much of a Deynen, but he was a good man. She went to get her cloak. It seemed she really would be able to give Teros the holiday he deserved after all. As she opened the door, he spoke one last time, not looking up from the workbench.

"You'll meet the caravan at the top of the hill in the city center, by the southwest lookout point. There's a statue there, of a soldier looking out toward the flats. I don't know if I'll be there or not to see you off, but if I'm not…good luck."

She nodded, closing the door behind her. This *was* her luck. All she needed now was the strength to see it done.

27

Serimh nodded to the palace guard, slipping down into the tunnels beneath the central tower. Despite a lifetime of science perfecting the shoddy chemistry in this basin, his request to use the Snow Father's altar felt like his first true stroke of genius. After all, inventions were really just a product of time and money, but *ideas* were the lifeblood of discovery.

He passed a few more guards on his way through the tunnels, and while they would surely report on his comings and goings, for the first time in years, he was left alone. With no zinc knight's shadow over his shoulder, they were letting him transport the supplies for the ceremony himself, afraid someone would comment if too many knights passed through the city center.

He turned back and forth through the narrow passages, angling himself toward the butler's staircase beneath the throne room. After passing his fourth set of guards, though, he stopped, counting in his head. *One. Two. Three.* A fifth set of guards crossed the passageway ahead of him. He'd memorized their rotations over the past few days, and those men walking by meant he was well and truly alone.

He ducked into an alcove in the hallway, dropping the box of serosine in his hands. He dug into his pockets, pulling out a bundle of jewelry and a dinner roll. Prying free a loose brick he'd opened in the wall, he stuffed everything inside.

It was nothing yet — not compared to the riches they'd tied up for him on the guild ledgers — but staring into the zinc king's eyes, he'd finally realized something. That money wasn't real. They may let him draw a bit of it if he succeeded with this round of serosine, but they'd never let him take it all. He had to be content with what he had, to escape with his meager little life. After all, if the science was what truly mattered, he'd find a way. He wouldn't exactly be spending money on a research staff if he was dead.

He put the brick back, scooping up his box and emerging from the alcove just as the guards turned back down the hallway. He nodded at them, though they barely paid him any mind. That was just as well. One day soon, he'd be back down in these tunnels to retrieve his things, and it'd be best if they ignored his passing. Finally, he reached the stairwell, finding the captain of the palace guard waiting for him there.

"Is that bloody it?" he asked, hands on hips. You could hardly see the man's face under his helm, his giant mustache large enough to make a bird's nest.

"This is it," Serimh said, placing the box along with another dozen lining the wall by the narrow stone stairs.

"Good. Tell your minders it ain't easy hiding all this. They certainly don't pay me enough for the trouble."

"I'll be sure to let them know," Serimh said, nodding earnestly. The captain immediately paled, his eyes widening.

"No, no, that won't be necessary. Only joking."

"Sure," Serimh said, smiling. "Only a joke."

He liked making this man uncomfortable, even if it had horrified him to realize how deeply in the pocket of the zinc knights the palace guard was. There were far too many corrupt men this side of the city, and it didn't bode well for the merchant council. Still, it wouldn't be his problem for much longer — not when he put this basin behind him forever.

"Any letters for me?"

It had been a risk, sending a letter through the central tower. It had been in code, of course, to one of his last old friends from the priesthood. Still, if he was leaving without all his money, he'd need somewhere to go. His friend had taken up with the crown in Yane — the weakest kingdom, though potentially the most likely to benefit from his services.

"There was one, actually," the captain said with a sly smile. "Figured I'd give it to the zinc knights, though, seeing as how it was *official* business and all."

By a miracle, Serimh kept his face passive, mirroring the other man's smile.

"As if those louts know how to read. Suppose I'll get it from them at the southern tower."

"Only joking again," the captain said, hastily pulling a letter from his pocket. Serimh opened it on the spot.

Lemon was all it said. It meant yes. He could come to Yane as soon as he was able.

"Thank you kindly, captain," Serimh said, handing him back the letter. "You can burn that for me."

"Uh, of course," the man said, putting the letter back in his pocket. Good. He'd left the captain thoroughly bewildered. Even if he thought Serimh was nothing more than the zinc king's pet, confusing him would keep him off the scent. Soldiers knew blades and helmets, but a man of science was apparently beyond their comprehension.

"Make sure you get some sleep, captain," Serimh said, leaving the stairwell. "Tomorrow will be a long day."

Of course, it would be longest for him. He'd no doubt finish it by slitting someone's throat, but what was a little more blood on his hands? After all, when he was done, he'd be *free*.

28

23ʳᵈ of Selomira 979
Rule of the Vindeista
(25ᵗʰ of Perat-kam, 985, 23ʳᵈ Year of Iron)

Eyri did as Chir said, buying an incredible amount of food. She even walked into the city center to the merchant's district and away from the meager choices in the Zinc Quarter. Since it was the night before the holiday, every stand was thronged with people, but she elbowed her way in all the same, buying yak tails, thrush reeds, and a mountain of potatoes. She even found a 'Zennan' hand-pie, though she could tell at a glance it wasn't from the sacred acres.

As she handed over the money — a fortune compared to the state of their finances only a few weeks ago — it felt absurd, sickening even. She felt like the other Masked Ones, the ones who'd feasted after every mission, gorging themselves on a toxic blend of privilege and suffering. Still, it wasn't for her own sake. It was for Teros. He…wouldn't take it well when he discovered she was leaving. She might not be able to make him see, but he deserved some sweetness before she went.

As she began the walk back to the mountains, though, she couldn't help but smile. She had done it. She had found the serosine, had finally found a way to redeem herself. And even if she failed, it was a chance, which felt like more than she'd had in a long while. For once, Deyn even looked beautiful to her, the mountains almost glistening against the dark blue sky. The sun felt *brighter* somehow — and perhaps it was, her workday ending earlier than it ever had since they'd arrived.

That feeling seemed to float her back to the cave, her shoulders barely even registering the weight of her bags as she climbed the steep path through the shale. She thought for a moment she might beat Teros back to the cave, but as she pulled back the moss, she could hear him shuffling inside. When she stuck her head through the other side, a smile on her face, Teros jumped, his eyes wide. There was something on his lap, but he threw it behind him, covering it with his shawl.

"What are you doing back so early?" he asked, standing as he rubbed his hands together.

"I'm off early for the holiday. What were *you* doing?"

"It's a surprise," he said quickly, glancing back at the large lump under his cloak. "I'll…finish it tomorrow before you wake up."

"Okay," she said, chuckling. "But I have a surprise too."

She held up the bag, patting it. A memory came back to her, though it was too vague to know if it was real. She could almost picture her father doing the same thing, coming home from the market before each bridge day laden with food. She couldn't picture his face any longer. In her mind, he looked like Borash, his beard scraggly and his clothes dirty. And her memories at the end, before her ascent, were full of hunger. But that smile…

She could tell Teros in the morning, couldn't she? Something in her wanted to hang onto this feeling, this…*lightness*. Teros had seemed better lately, not whispering to himself as much or crying out in his sleep. There was enough time for worry later; tonight should be a celebration. Of course, that was assuming she could think of anything but the task before her…

She sat beside Teros, starting on the potatoes as he dressed the meat. She flipped over their pot lid to use as a cutting board. When she pulled her knife from her boot, though, she thought of the serosine again. She knew basically nothing of Chir's request — how many people she'd be traveling with, whether or not there would be knights. Still, she pictured herself on a boat, the quiet darkness of the river surrounding her.

She felt the wood beneath her feet, stepping between the boards to keep them from creaking. There were flickering flames on the bow, shining against the crags of the cavern above. The serosine was in the middle of the barge, hidden beneath a tarp, the sailors giving it a wide berth. Should she just dump it in the river? She didn't know how deep the water was, but surely it would be impossible to find in the darkness. She could kill the crew, but then how would she make it back to Teros? She would do it if she had to, though she didn't relish losing her way in the caverns, wandering like a cave witch until she starved or drowned or—

"You can drop them in the pot when they're cut," Teros said, gesturing to her potatoes. "We'll just stew the meat with the vegetables to keep things easy."

She looked down at the lid, finding a tiny mountain of quartered potatoes. She could hardly remember cutting them, her hands moving on their own.

"Alright," she said, her mouth dry. Maybe she should have bought some wine, something to keep her mind from racing. She shook her head, focusing on Teros. "How was the village today?"

He started chattering about Hv'rano. It felt like he was describing a play she'd never seen, rattling off a cast of characters she didn't know. Still, the shower of happy words seemed to calm her. She did little more than nod along to his story, but it kept her anchored to the present, to her last night with this precious boy.

She started cutting the potatoes again with purpose. This meal would be the only gift she could give him until she found the serosine, until she took him home. She was no cook — and wasn't exactly sure if how you cut potatoes really mattered — but she did it all the same, the quarters becoming perfect as she focused on them.

Maybe cutting potatoes wasn't much, but it suddenly seemed essential. Before she disappointed Teros, she would have him know how much she loved him. With time, he might even look back at this meal and smile, forgiving her for what she'd had to do. After all, that's what her family had done for her. Even decades after they sold her, she could still picture those smiles, the memory sweet enough to last through all her tears.

————

Long after Eyri left, Chir still sat alone in the smithy, staring at Sonote's sword. *Vandraeb* glittered in the darkness, his own hazy reflection on the blade barely visible in the lamplight. He tried to make out his face, but it seemed foreign, a man he no longer recognized. A man…who could kill a friend. But what choice did he have? The king had to be destroyed, and he was out of cards to play. Even if the girl didn't deserve to die, wouldn't thousands die when Iremi nal Miri finally got his war?

After she'd left, he'd sent for one of the zinc king's knights, confirming he had a proper candidate. When he'd reached out to them that morning, they'd been desperate for him to commit on the spot, certain they needed to try and finish this on Baker's Day. Still, he wouldn't be rushed. He'd wanted to talk to Eyri first, and he had, confirming what he needed to know about her boy.

Unfortunately, their answer had been swift. Eyri was the one they wanted. Of course, it made him wonder how many other candidates they'd had. If the holiday came and went without a Zennan's blood, would the king's plans be set back? Perhaps it didn't matter. The king would have his war with or without the blood magic. Either way, Chir refused to miss his chance. If he made First Quartermaster, he'd have the entire council in his hands.

At least he'd paid the girl well. He'd given Eyri enough money for a hundred meals — not that it gave him much solace now. Still, it was only right, her son soon to be forced to live without her. More than food, the money would be enough to join a guild — even for a foreigner. The boy could start over. After all, how many loved ones had *he* been forced to live without? His father, his son…*Sonote*. Life was just a series of losings, a never-ending affront from the gods. He chuckled — a dry, sad sound in the darkness of the shop — remembering what his mentor used to say.

"The gods are just a forge, boy. They can't help it if they burn their children."

Perhaps that was simply the way of existence, but at least in Deyn they knew the truth — even as the gods destroyed your life from the inside out, it was still yours to use. After all, that was the point of the guilds, wasn't it? Even if the gods were a forge, humans were the blades, sharp enough to kill no matter what they'd been through. Maybe Eyri's boy would even come and work for him after his mother died.

He pictured it then, the boy standing in the door to the smithy, his head haloed in light. He'd be filled with grief and rage like Sonote once was, his eyes aflame. And in the wake of his mother's sacrifice, perhaps he'd want to fight at Chir's side. Perhaps he'd want to learn the sword, to turn the wreckage of his life into a flame. It wasn't much, but it was a *chance*. The only sickening thing was knowing he'd accept the boy's help if it meant vengeance.

He finally got up, his back protesting as he reached up to hang the sword above the door. It would be an early morning, and he ought to try — or at least *pretend* — to get some sleep. He hadn't decided until that very moment, but he would be there in the morning. Not for the ceremony — he refused to dignify that bloody serosine with his presence — but for the girl. She deserved to hear it from his own lips what he was doing. And at the end, maybe he could give her the solace the king had denied him, a chance to promise her the boy would be alright.

He locked the door, heading toward home, its lights already visible on the hill beside the falls. An empty home was a poor beacon for a man fumbling in the dark, but at least he had a direction again. It was a curse, this path he'd chosen, but it was better than being a *spo'gimes*. Perhaps that was all heaven was, the end of your to-do list, a sun setting on a broken spirit. But for now, at least, he still lived. He knew what he wanted, and he would have it, no matter how much blood stood between him and the king.

29

1ˢᵗ of Curis-gan, 970, 8ᵗʰ Year of Iron
17ᵗʰ Day of the War - 'The Breaking'
Fifteen Years Ago

Viden crossed the barren field, weaving between pockets of soldiers as he looked for Curan. For some cursed reason, he was thinking of the Wise Father, as if a bloody priest's poem could describe the desolation all around him. Still, there was one line that kept coming back to him — *war is fire and men the fodder.* It was about the Giant Lands, of course — and the persecution of the old gods — but even after a thousand years, it seemed nothing had changed. War was still a fire, and here they were, burning.

He finally found her sitting on a patch of moss, staring at Sen'el'tul, its bald peak the only thing visible beyond the sea of smoke before them. It had only been two days since the attack — what the humans were starting to call the 'Day of the Hawk' — but it felt like a year. After Bitan's funeral and a night full of bonfires, the hills echoing with dirges, it felt like they'd never stopped fighting. They'd killed thousands of soldiers and dozens of knights, more than five meeting their end on Curan's blade. They were…exhausted. But at least it would be over soon. Once they broke the wall of serosine protecting what was left of the Deynen army, the city and its dam wouldn't be far behind.

"Curan," he said gently, crouching behind her. He touched her shoulder, but she didn't move, the slow rising of her chest the only sign she was alive. He almost thought she'd fallen asleep sitting up when she spoke, her voice little more than a whisper.

"Can I come back here? At the end?"

Unfortunately, he knew exactly what she meant. He could feel the Passing creeping closer himself, the hundreds — no, *thousands* — of chul'uns they'd burned seeping into his bones. They'd already lost dozens of Masked Ones in the counterattack, not to mention what they'd lose before the day was done. He wanted to cry, thinking of Curan dying someday, but what could be done? The Passing came for them all. At least he deserved his fate. He'd thought this time would be different, but he was no father to her. He was only her keeper, another man condemning her to die. All he could do was ease her passage.

"Sure," he said, rubbing the back of her head over the straps of her mask. "With enough dandelion, you can go anywhere you like. It's a nice view."

He looked at the mountain with her for another moment, ignoring the whistles of the sergeants calling them to the front line.

"Come on," he finally said, standing as he gave her his hand. "It's time."

The Masked Ones started forming up on a rise above the Deynens, their entire army jammed into their base at Sesarin. The enemy — a mix of knights and soldiers — was huddled up around their huge serosine spikes, as if they could protect the metal with their swords. Unfortunately for them, someone had realized a Masked One could break serosine if they threw enough power at it. The spikes around their camp were massive, rising some fifteen feet in the air, but they would break them today, whatever it cost.

As they passed the human ranks of the Zennan army, he could see the doubt in their eyes. When these men had signed up, they hadn't thought it possible for a Masked One to die. Even going to war, they'd probably thought death a distant thing. After all, weren't the Deynens just a bunch of peasant farmers? But now they knew how wrong they'd been, knew how much they had to fear. If this attack failed and the Masked Ones were pushed back again, these men would be the first to die.

Despite the risks, the Iron King was at the front, sitting atop a massive horse, his sword in hand. His eyes were ablaze with hate, the dark light never leaving them since he'd put his son's body on the pyre. It seemed he, at least, would ride into the Deynen lines alone if he had to. He was ending this war today, no matter which side the Zennans ended up on.

The line of Masked Ones finally formed. The sergeants kept blowing their whistles, but no one needed orders. Everyone knew what to do. Viden dropped into a fighting stance, Curan copying him as he summoned all the Passion he could muster. The air around them seemed to cool as they pooled their fire, their breath becoming fog. The power boiled in his stomach, each of them having swallowed pepper oil until they wanted to vomit. But even if none of them ever summoned fire again, it would be because they'd found a lifetime of power in this place.

Somewhere along the line, someone began to sing. The voice was low, more like a growl, but quickly, others joined him in the dismal chorus. It was the *Song of Curses*, the Wise Father heaping evil on his enemies as he rode into the desert, his home in flames behind him. The song had always seemed bleak to him, a greater indictment of the Masked Ones than the giants they'd left behind. Still, as the fire welled up in his chest, the Passing burning his mind, he found himself singing along.

"You are your own destruction!" he roared along with the others, the first fireball finally forming above his head.

Soon, a wall of flames appeared in the air. Curan's was even larger than his, and he heard her singing too, her tiny voice completely out of step with the liquid rage rippling above her. Finally, their voices reaching a crescendo, they let the fire go, the Passion arcing across the sky. As it hit the serosine, the ground shook, the sky seeming to groan with thunder as the air shimmered and clapped shut again. Somehow, though, the serosine held. He almost lost hope then, almost grabbed Curan to run, but then he saw it — a giant crack in the middle of the nearest spike.

He wanted to gag, the bile rising in his throat, but instead he sang, choking it down as they summoned their flames again. The tiredness building inside him the past few days sunk deeper into his bones, but it was nothing compared to his fury. The Passing called to him, urging him to burn himself out, anything to take the lives of his enemies. He called another fireball, the air splitting as he sang.

THE END OF PART THREE

The Song of Curses

—:—

Woe to the men who spat on gods,
and woe the children born them.
With mighty fire, I shall return
the desert's burn forgotten.

You see, I've dreamed a mighty dream,
the goddess whispers in my ear.
I've seen the shores of further seas,
and the fish that swim among them.

Your ships they may have sailed the skies,
your riches your seduction.
For even with your throne of jewels,
you are your own destruction.

For even if a thousand years
should pass behind my warning.
It is *my* vengeance you should fear,
my coming with the morning.

You've worshipped at an evil art,
and chased the weak with wicked blades.
The Sacred Mother, Entodai
will forever curse your wicked ways.

PART FOUR

A Journal

Everything destroyed. Everything I built. The dam, the metal, all of it gone. Still, by some curse of the gods, I'm not free. A knight came to find me in the wreckage. It seems someone's killed the king in a duel. The new king seems a boy really, just a lad from the First Zamak named Iremi nal Miri. He says I'll be needed, which means I'm being watched again. Of course, in many ways, I still want to help. The people are near to starving, and we'll need more spikes to survive the winter. I only wonder, when I'm done, will there ever be a way out?

-Journal of Serimh nal Akistore:
964th Year of Finding, 18th of Sitamira

—:—

30

Eyri woke early the next morning, her mind still full of dreams. As she stared at the ceiling of the cave, they slipped away, leaving only a vague impression behind. Something from the war, her time with Viden. Would he be proud of her now? He'd taught her everything, of course, but then he'd told her to run. But what would running do? Who was she without the mask? Still, she closed her eyes, picturing his eyes under his mask, his smile. Even if her life would disappoint him now, she'd need his strength for what was coming.

She rolled over, finding Teros gone, though she heard him working by the fire. She sighed, sitting up. It was probably for the best. As much as she wanted to hold him one last time, she should be dressed before she told him. He might not take it well, and she wanted to be ready to leave as soon as possible. She may well need time to console him, though she couldn't — *wouldn't* — miss her opening with Chir.

She dressed slowly, her plain white clothes from Hv'rano seeming strange now. After months of drudgery, she had to see them through the lens of battle, each fold suddenly a potential liability. She wrapped and rewrapped her tunic, stretching out her arms as she tried tucking the cloth into her belt in different ways until her range of motion felt right. Finally, with her boots laced and her shawl around her shoulders, she picked up her sword. Freeing it from its scabbard, she held it in both hands, watching its mercury amalgam in the growing light.

"One more time, old friend."

She put it on her belt, walking from the cave with her head held high. Teros was by the fire, his head down as he fiddled with something in his lap.

"Teros," she said, the name sounding strange for some reason, as if she'd rehearsed it too many times.

He looked up, eyebrows raised. He would be fine. Even if he worried now, he would be grateful when she saved them, when she freed them from this place.

"I finished it!" he said, holding up the basket he'd been weaving. It was a bit misshapen, but it was a wonder he'd gotten all that grass to turn into anything at all. It might fall apart from a single prick of the knife, but it was still charming, covered in flowers. Teros stood, handing it to her.

"They make these in Hv'rano for Baker's Day. I made one for my friend Liska, too, but I thought…you could join us? The whole village goes into town, and the bakers hand out all sorts of sweets at the parade. You—"

"Teros," she said firmly, taking him by the shoulder. "I have to tell you something." She put her basket by the other one, easing him down as they sat by the fire. A pit formed in her stomach. They'd had a feast the night before, of course, but she hadn't really thought about the holiday — or Teros wanting her to join him. Still, he would understand when he knew the truth. He had to.

"I think I found the serosine. Chir invited me to leave the basin with some kind of shipment, and I'm going to see if I can destroy it. But—" She almost mentioned not coming back, the risk of her failure, but she swallowed the words. "But…while I'm gone, I want you to stay in the village. Ask one of your friends at school if you can stay with them. I'll feel better knowing you aren't alone."

"You…found it?" he asked. He shook his head, looking at the ground. He whispered the next words, as if saying them to himself. "I didn't think you would."

Whispered or not, the words were like a lance through her chest. She'd been struggling, true, but did he really think her such a failure?

"You didn't think I could?"

"No, no," Teros said, looking up as he frowned. "It's not like that. I guess…I *hoped* you wouldn't."

"But we need this, Teros. How else do I get you home?"

He stared at the ground, his cheek bulging as he clenched his jaw. He opened his mouth before closing it again, his breathing quick as he tried to speak.

"Eyri…" he finally got out. "We *are* home." He met her eyes, his face tortured like he'd never smile again. "You and me, *together*. Even if you get the serosine, do you really think they'll just let us come back? And what if… What if I lose you? You can't go."

Suddenly, she was on her feet, her hand on her sword. Teros stared at the hilt, just noticing it on her belt.

"I have to go," she said. She reached for his shoulder before thinking better of it. "Don't worry, alright? Everything will be fine. I can do this."

She started for the exit, hoping she could avoid an argument, but he ran up behind her, throwing his arms around her waist.

"No," he moaned, his breath ragged as he began to cry. "Please don't."

She took his arms, managing to turn as she patted his back, unable to hug him properly with his head buried in her stomach. Was he just worried about her, then? It was a risk, true, but she had to do *something*. She wouldn't let him waste his life living in a cave when she had a chance to get him home. He started whispering to himself, his breath hot against her robes as he muttered a dozen words in the span of a heartbeat.

"Teros," she said gently, taking him by the chin as she lifted his head. "I have to do this. I have to get you home."

"You're wrong," he said, gritting his teeth as he met her eyes. "I know bad things happened to you, Eyri, but you don't have to do this to have a life. We don't have to go home to have a life. We're happy *now*. We're safe *now*. Don't throw that away. We aren't Masked Ones anymore."

Maybe he wasn't. But what was she? She was a sword with no mask. A magician with no magic. A mother…with someone else's child.

"I know you're happy," she said, finally admitting it to herself, a tear coming to her eye. "But what am I here, Teros? I'm nothing without Zenn, don't you see that? Don't you *want* to go back?"

"No," he said, taking a step away from her. "There's nothing back there."

"But it's our home. If we don't care about Zenn, what was it all for? The training, the dying. Why did I live this life? Why did I live at all? This isn't real, Teros. We don't belong here."

"And we belong in Zenn?" he asked, his face suddenly dark as he let her go. "They killed my mother. They killed Borash. You think we *belong* with them? They're evil, Eyri. I wish I could change it, but I can't." He sucked in a breath, looking at the sky. "Why can't you just live? You're alive because you deserve to be, we both do. If we didn't, then why did you run? Why did you save me?"

Why did she save him? For Borash? For herself? She'd held her own mask in her hand and cracked it in half. She'd broken her own shackles, but what was she without them?

"I don't know," she said. It was the truth, but Teros clamped his eyes shut, squeezing out fresh tears.

"I know they hurt you," he said, his voice shaking, "but you're a good person. Even when you came to me in the tower, you were *kind*. Don't let them have you, Eyri. Zenn doesn't matter."

She sucked in a breath, swallowing her words. Part of her wanted to remind him of how he used to feel, when he'd wanted to help Zenn, change it. But could she really blame him? He didn't have to make the choices she made. Wasn't that his point? Why else did she save him?

"It matters to me," she said instead, and she found she meant it. Finally, all her months of indecision had led to clarity. He was right, Zenn did need to change. The magic was *not* the mask. Borash had proven that. Teros had proven that. But she found she couldn't let go. She couldn't abandon everything she'd sacrificed for, even if it needed changing. She hated herself for what she'd done in the temple, even if she wouldn't take it back. There had to be another way. She had to find another way.

"I have to go, Teros. I have to make this right. Stay with your friends; I'll come back when I can."

She cupped his cheek, taking a deep breath as she turned away. She lifted the moss cover on the cavern, ducking through the crack in the rocks. Still, she couldn't help but hear him crying behind her, the beautiful, brilliant boy who would never be truly hers.

———

"Please, please, please," Teros muttered, his eyes clamped shut. But who was he praying to? And why did he think they would listen? If it was Mother, he'd already failed her. All she'd wanted was for him to be safe, for them to stay together, but he'd lost Eyri, driven her away. He'd thought he was doing the right thing, starting a life here, but he'd left Eyri out of it, making her feel like the only thing she was good for was the serosine.

Even worse, she couldn't take him with her. He'd failed at his training, too, still useless with a sword even after all these months. What if he'd tried harder? What if he'd focused on the sword instead of Deynen? Even if he couldn't convince her to stay, he could have at least tried to be helpful, tried to keep her alive. Now she would die, and it was all his fault.

"No," he groaned. "No, no, no."

He was squatting now, his arms around his legs, his face buried in his knees. He wanted to be smaller, wanted to disappear. Eyri was gone, and he had done nothing to stop her. He *was* nothing.

Together, a voice whispered in his mind, but he knew it was a lie. He'd whispered that word to himself a thousand times since the Day of Joy, and what had it gotten him?

Together, the voice whispered again, more urgently. Whose voice was it? Mother's? Someone else? Was he hearing things or was it some new ghost, ready to plague his mind? It was a woman's voice, but she sounded far away. Still, the way she spoke…it felt like home. He squeezed his eyes shut tighter, the tears pushing out between his eyelids.

"Together," he whispered, echoing the voice. His mind was suddenly full of whispers, and he could feel the earth around him as if it were spinning, the stone of the mountains no longer solid, like it had become a part of the wind.

Maybe he could still help Eyri. Useless with the sword or not, if he went with her now, he could try, he could show her that he cared. Maybe then she'd see, and she wouldn't have to go. And if she still did… Well, at least he would be there to help her — or die by her side. But it was better than staying here, crouching in an empty home with a mind full of whispers.

He got up before he lost his nerve, running after Eyri. He left the moss open on the door and the fire burning, but it didn't matter. He had to catch Eyri before it was too late, before he lost her forever.

31

Eyri reached the meeting place, finding the statue Chir had mentioned. It was a soldier made of bronze, looking out toward the flats where so many had died. But even with all that loss, war was coming again, as if they'd all forgotten what the first one cost them. There was a tree next to the statue, just coming into bloom, its dark-red petals like blood as they blew into the wind. It was a strange place to meet, and oddly quiet for the Eighth Ward. There was a sort of half-alley to her right, with one side facing the backs of buildings while the other ended in a fence at the edge of the cliff.

You could see for miles to the south and west, though, and she leaned against the fence, looking in the direction of Hv'rano. Would Teros forgive her? Already, she burned with shame for snapping at him — and even worse, for making him snap at her. He was such a mild boy, but the fury in his eyes… Perhaps it was for the best. It was just another sign that she was right. She was useless to him as she was now. She was no mother, and unless she found her purpose, she would only do more harm.

She heard the click of hooves behind her and turned, finding Chir atop a giant horse. It had to be from Seln, a war horse, the kind she remembered from the fighting. So Chir really did have contacts in the army… He raised a hand, and she walked over, stopping just out of range.

"Ready for the trip?" he asked. She wasn't sure if she'd see him again — had honestly hoped she wouldn't — but perhaps he was only here to send her off. She'd kill him if she had to, but she'd rather he didn't join them.

"I am."

He pointed at the sword in her left hand. "You look like exactly what we'll need. Is that Zennan?"

"Yes," she said. "It was my father's, he was a palace guard."

That was the lie she'd cooked up. At least it would explain the hilt, though she'd have to be careful not to show her amalgam if she ever had to pull the blade. Still, they couldn't pretend to be friends forever. The moment she had a chance at the serosine, she'd take it.

"Where's the shipment?" she asked. She thought they'd have wagons, but the alley was empty, with nothing on the corner of the main street.

"Just needed to size you up first," he said. He turned his horse to the side as he put his fingers to his lips, letting out a sharp whistle. "I liked you, lass. Between us, I really hope you put up a fight."

She frowned, whipping her head around as she heard more horses behind her. Suddenly, there were four knights on the street, a hooded man between them.

"What—" she began to ask Chir, but the old man had backed away, replaced by four soldiers emerging from the alley.

Her mind raced. How had they discovered who she was? What would they do to her? She'd never imagined the Deynens giving her up to Zenn, least of all with all that serosine. Unless they weren't giving her up… She pulled her sword, the mercury casting light onto the cobblestones. The soldiers had been trying to surround her, but they stopped, they—

"Eyri?"

She spun, finding Teros behind her. Looking between her and the knights, he had just climbed the hill, stopping as he reached the edge of the fence. The hooded man looked right at her, her heart sinking.

"Megre nes barihbna," he said, turning to the knights.

She knew what that meant, at least. Such a simple sentence, its meaning haunting. *The child would be better.* This was no arrest.

"Run!" she screamed, Teros's eyes widening. But even as time seemed to slow, she was helpless to stop what was happening. One of the knights was already off his horse, grabbing Teros like a sack of grain. She reached for her belt knife, prepared to put it through the knight's eye, but she heard the soldiers moving behind her and knew she had no choice. She'd have to fight them all, have to cut her way to Teros.

She spun, swinging hard, the nearest soldier's eyes widening as her sword split his throat.

"Anndem," one of them whispered. *Demon.* Good. They knew what she was, and if they took her boy, that's what they would get.

The remaining soldiers snapped out of their shock, surrounding her. She looked over her shoulder, hoping there was still time, but the knights were riding away, the one who'd taken Teros draping the boy over his saddle.

The soldier in front of her was already swinging, his massive broadsword dropping in an arc. She got her sword up in time, but he hit hard, the sword dropping from her hands with a clang. Still, he'd swung too hard, committed too much. Before he could get his sword up again, she jabbed with her empty sword hand, collapsing his windpipe.

Still, she knew she had no time, knew she had to fight the others. She freed her belt knife, blocking the next soldier's swing with the hilt. She twisted the blade from his hands, pulling him to the ground as he lost his balance. She didn't have time to grab her own sword, but she balled her fists tight, slamming them into his face again and again. She felt only fury, a searing fire in her heart, each blow a single thought. *They. Had. Teros.*

The final soldier reached her, grabbing her by the hair in a panic. He dragged her backwards, pulling her off his friend. The other man was hurt badly, but he forced an eye open, scrambling for his sword. She screamed, arching her back as she put everything into a kick, the soldier's skull giving off a sharp crack as her boot connected. They both fell into a heap, the side of her head smashing into the cobblestones.

Her vision swam, but she got to her feet, beating the injured soldier to his blade. As she slit his throat, she heard a thunder of hooves, Chir galloping from the alley in the direction the knights had gone.

"No!" she screamed. The knife flew from her hand, taking the old man in the back. He fell from his saddle, the horse rearing up as it realized it had lost its rider. She grabbed her sword, sprinting toward Chir despite the ringing in her ears. She rolled him over, his eyes glassy as blood spilled from his mouth.

"Where?!" she shouted, slapping him.

He coughed, meeting her eyes.

"The tower," he said, his voice soft. She got up to take the horse, but he grabbed her wrist.

"I'm sorry," he said. "They wanted…a Zennan. But. The boy… I didn't… Like…Sonote…"

"It's alright," she felt herself saying with the last human part of her left. "It's alright." She slit his throat, the only quick death she could give him in the time she had as she ran toward his horse.

If only she hadn't come here. If only she'd listened. She didn't know what these men were planning, but what plan could be worth the life of her child? And what of hers? She'd been so obsessed with finding the serosine, with becoming someone again, that she'd traded Teros's life for it.

And for what? A king who wanted her dead? A kingdom that had imprisoned her? Teros was *good,* and he was hers. *Had* been hers… But she would throw away this life if it meant having him back. It was useless without him anyway. But was she strong enough? Perhaps she wasn't, but her old self was. The woman still inside the mask. The woman who would save that boy.

732 threw herself into the saddle, kicking the horse toward the tower. She would reach him before it was too late, even if it meant killing every soldier in her way.

———

Teros opened his eyes, though the searing pain in his forehead made him close them again. Where was he? Even with the thunder of hooves beneath him, it took him a moment. *Eyri.* He almost looked for her — whatever direction that was — but he didn't dare move, even as it filled him with shame. The moment they took him, he'd tried to break free, had even tried to grab the knight's sword, but he'd been hit so hard on the head he'd blacked out.

There were no whispers in his mind now, only a deep river of emptiness. He was in the dark now, his only candle burnt through. If only he'd listened. If only he hadn't made Eyri so unhappy. He'd burdened her, had left her so alone she'd rather put herself in danger than go on living with him. But now, even if she escaped those soldiers, he knew she'd come for him, knew she'd fight those knights without her magic…

He thought about trying to roll from the saddle, but the knight's hand was heavy on his back, pinning him against the horse. Besides, would he even survive the fall? Perhaps it didn't matter so long as it stopped them from getting to their destination. There were witnesses here, places for Eyri to hide.

But no. He was trapped, and he was useless.

Please, he prayed, though he wasn't sure to who. Mother? The old gods? The magic was gone, and maybe he and Eyri with it. So not the Wise Father, then, but to who? An image of a woman came to his mind. She was beautiful, half his mother, half not. She sat by an impossible amount of water, like a thousand ponds in one. She smiled warmly, like she saw his soul and wasn't disgusted by it.

Please, he thought again, reaching for the woman with his voice. Maybe it was the Sacred Mother. Maybe he was dying. His head was so fuzzy, he couldn't seem to tell the difference. But he would pray for all he was worth, and hopefully, Eyri would survive.

32

732 flew through the city like an arrow. Her horse foamed against the bit, but it obeyed, a true Deynen war horse. Luckily for her, it didn't care what kind of war it was riding into. A few shopkeepers looked out at her as she passed, but the city was strangely quiet. It seemed they'd picked Baker's Day on purpose, everyone long since headed to the First Ward to celebrate. Which only made her curse herself more. How long had this been planned? How high did it go? The presence of those knights alone was a bad sign. With no witnesses on the streets, how much time did she really have?

And what could they possibly want with Teros? Even as it paled in comparison to the power of the Masked Ones, Deynen magic was strange, arcane. She'd heard rumors of blood magic, but that only filled her with more terror. She ground her teeth, an image of Teros's throat being slit forcing its way into her mind. It felt like the temple all over again, this wonderful, irreplaceable boy sacrificed at an altar she had no power to destroy. She pushed the horse harder, feeling already like she was weeks too late.

As she burst into the central square, the tower loomed above her. There were more guards than usual, a half-dozen at least, and they spotted her, shouting as they pointed at her horse. She could fight six, but how many more inside? How many could she drop before the zinc knights found her? If only she had magic! She pushed her horse directly through the center of the pillars, tempted to curse the gods for abandoning her, for abandoning Teros. But she couldn't find the words. Weak as she was, she'd need the gods now. Would they come to her like they had in the temple? Or would they curse her for what she'd done, trading a wonderful boy for her pride?

"Save him!" she shouted at the pillars as she rode between them. Even if they refused her plea, the gods *would* hear her. Even if she died, she would fall as a pillar of flame, reminding the Elders — and any other bastard in the pantheon — of how they'd failed her. They could look down from their precious mountain at a river of blood for all she cared. Forget the gods. Forget the binds of life. She would unbind herself and her sword would swing free.

732 slammed her horse into the first two guards, the mount not caring for

their palace livery in its frenzy, its hooves cracking bones as the soldiers dropped. She swung from the saddle, tapping the side of the horse's head so it would fight on the right as she took the soldiers on the left. Thankfully, it was trained the same as a Zennan mount, and it obeyed, leaving her with only two to fight. She whirled between them, beheading one in a powerful swing, her sword coming through to clang against the soldier's on the other side.

"Anndem!" he cried, dashing back with his sword held before him. *"Anndem!"*

Her horse returned as the tower doors opened, the giant metal entrance groaning as more soldiers pushed through. Good that they knew her for what she was. Their fear would make quick work. And perhaps she did look the part of a demon. She could feel her hair slick with blood from where her head had slammed against the ground, and she'd earned more than a few cuts on her arms. But for once, her mind felt clear. This was something she could do. Even without her mask, she knew what she was. She was death, and she would show these men their end.

She swung into the saddle, rearing the horse up. The guards from inside the tower, a dozen this time, saw her and seemed to change their minds. One tried to pull the door closed again, but he was too late. It was open, and she was coming through.

———

Serimh pushed up the stairs of the tower, a pit forming in his stomach as he tried to avoid looking behind him. Still, short of stuffing his ears, it was impossible to ignore the struggling child, squirming despite the massive arms of the knight holding him. He almost regretted taking the boy. Would he really be able to slit his throat? The knights could do that part, of course, but if they botched the blood magic…

He curled his hands into fists, grinding his teeth. Damn it all! He'd have to do it himself. It was the only thing standing between him and freedom, between him and the life he deserved. And the child *would* be powerful. He'd seen the woman's sword and there was no doubt who she was. You'd have to be a fool not to put two and two together — all anyone could talk about was that fight at the Zennan temple all those months ago.

Luckily, the knights hadn't seemed to notice. They weren't used to thinking for themselves, of course, but they hadn't called for help yet. His minders were young, perhaps even young enough to have dodged the war, but who didn't know a demon sword on sight? Still, it was for the best. The last thing he needed was more bastards from the army here. If only he could be sure the woman was dead… He didn't want to be disturbed, let alone what she might do to them if she still lived.

Most importantly, he didn't want to lose this precious blood. It was his ticket out of Deyn, the only way the knights would ignore him long enough for his escape. But if they realized what the boy really was, the fools on the throne would have their own designs, some new way to imprison him forever. He just had to act quickly, had to—

He heard shouting from below, the guards who'd been so placid before now crying for their lives.

"Culo 'fd," he cursed under his breath, turning to the knights. "We need to hurry. The woman must have help."

He pointed to the knight in the back.

"Go help the guards. You three, follow me, and give me the boy. We're doing this ceremony now."

———

732 faced five soldiers, the last ones left, the men's eyes wide with fear as they backed themselves into a knot. There were some two dozen dead around them, the inside of the tower covered in blood so dark it swallowed up the torchlight. Her breathing was heavy but her heart still raced, every second pounding with fresh urgency. The knights hadn't shown themselves yet — her initial attack exploding like Passion itself — but she was clearly losing time. And as her time diminished, her doubt only grew.

She could see in her periphery that she was covered in blood. Even if only part of it was her own, it held a simple truth: she was no Masked One. She had fought as well as a human possibly could, but her magic was gone. And with it, she had taken more hits than she had in years. Her arms were scored with cuts and her wrists ached, the sword growing heavy and her vision blurred. But if she wasn't 732, could Eyri finished this? Could anyone? She had come this far on rage alone, but it was hard to know if she could push through what was ahead.

Still, she loved Teros. That fact was undeniable. It made her think of Viden again, the man giving everything to protect her. Even if he was as broken as she was, even if it hadn't saved his life, he'd never faltered. And she would do the same. Even if she couldn't give Teros a good life and stay alive, perhaps she could offer him one in leaving, destroying everything in her path until he was free.

Suddenly, she remembered being a child, Borash appearing in her mind. The girl she'd been felt distant, that girl's laughter foreign. But if she *was* Eyri, that woman was only six years old, her time in the mask a gaping hole in the center of her life. But perhaps there was power in that. She wasn't a woman, she was a *void.* She was the blackness in the caves, devoid of life but full of power. And even as it had made her a terrible mother, it made her something more. It made her a *sword.*

The Void moved in, no longer afraid. Death was simple; she only needed to guarantee it was a good one. As she took the first soldier in the neck, the others seemed to realize the weakness in their defenses. Their swords were nothing to her, and even facing outward, they couldn't keep her out. They panicked, trying to form a new shape, but it was too late. She dropped them one by one, with only the last of them escaping through the open door.

She heard steps on the stairs behind her and turned, throwing her knife. It took a zinc knight in the eye, his armor clanging as he fell against the stone.

Lucky. Even with all her practice, it was a once-in-a-lifetime throw. Perhaps luck was the only thing the gods were willing to give her now, but she probably wouldn't get that lucky again. Surprise never lasted, and there were at least three more knights somewhere above, marching Teros toward whatever evil they were planning.

The Void stepped over the knight, beginning the climb deeper into the tower. She thought about taking his sword. It *was* magic, after all, but it was heavy too, and she didn't know how to use it. She would have to use her own sword, and perhaps a bit more luck if she could get it. It was something, even if it was all she had.

———

She found the knights on the next floor, hurrying with Teros and the hooded man toward the next set of stairs. It was a strange building, the second floor empty save for a huge bank of windows facing the pillars in the square. She hoped the gods were watching, hoped they'd hear her prayers.

"Stop!" she yelled in Zennan, unable to think through her paltry Deynen with the blood pulsing in her ears. Still, the knights stopped, turning with their hands on swords. It seemed she'd genuinely taken them by surprise, their eyes widening. The hooded man had already reached the steps — one hand on Teros's collar while another held a knife to his throat — but he froze as he saw her, staring.

One of the knights barked an order, and the three of them formed into a hasty triangle in the middle of the room. She had no magic of her own to parry with, of course, but she knew this formation well — had killed plenty of knights trying to use it to fend her off. The ones on the side would use wind to create a barrier while the knight in the middle moved in to fight her with his sword. Already, there was a shift in the room, the air pressure drawing toward those men as they drew their blades. It would be hard to see the wind coming, but not impossible. Like that day in the valley, she could just catch a glimpse of Identity on the air, a glimmer of what was to come. She could do this.

She darted in, only just feeling the change in the air as the first blast of wind came in. She slid beneath it just in time, the tower groaning as it hit the walls on the other side, the pressure clapping closed behind it like thunder. She came up in a swing, already facing the knight in the center. That could buy her some time on the wind — she was too close to their comrade now — but that also meant she'd have to be ready for three swords.

Still, these men and their swords were huge, and one was problem enough. Her first swing missed his neck by an inch, but he parried, their swords meeting with a huge clang, the vibration shaking her arm. Fortunately for her, in the case of Deynen knights, big also meant slow. She ducked his next swing, scoring a gash on his knee in the gap between the plate. He swore, but that was all she could do, pushed back as the knight on her right came in, forcing her to roll as he swung for her back.

She was on the side nearest Teros now, but it was too soon to try and reach him. They'd both be destroyed by the wind in seconds if they ran, and it wasn't like they could hide inside this tower. Even worse, she could sense all of Deyn around her like a vise, already feeling the need to be gone before more knights poured down on them. The knights rotated their triangle, putting a new knight in the center. It was another tactic she knew — keeping any one knight from becoming too weak — but it was also a way they drew out fights, using time she didn't have.

This time, she ran for the man she'd already wounded on her right. He was already mid-swing with a torrent of wind, aiming it lower to the ground this time. But instead of ducking, she *jumped,* feeling the ripple in the air beneath her. She kicked off the wind itself, redirecting herself toward the new man in the center, surprising him as she earned a slash under his helm — albeit not a lethal one.

The others were ready for her this time, and they moved in more quickly, not leaving a one-on-one fight to chance. Still, the one with the wound on his knee was slower, and she parried the knight on her left, backing away before they could trap her. But how long could she keep this up? Even if she scored one hit in each exchange, it would take too long to bleed them out.

She spared a glance for the stairs, the hooded man still standing there with Teros, the knife still at his throat. Teros met her eyes, mouthing something she couldn't make out. She felt herself growl, everything in her wanting to kill that man. But he would want her to lose her cool, was no doubt hoping she'd slip up. As she watched, the man ducked, pulling Teros down behind the stairs.

She turned just in time for the next bout of wind, preparing to jump. But they'd thrown their gale in an X, one knight going high while the other went low. It took her in the knees, flipping her over. She threw out an arm to keep her head from hitting the stone but she slammed into the ground all the same, the pain like lightning.

Somehow, she'd held onto her sword, though it thrummed in her hand. Did that mean she'd broken her arm? She— *Her amalgam.* The sword was humming with Identity, somehow stealing some of the wind's strength and pulling it into her sword. She couldn't see it exactly — her powers were still too weak without food — but she could *feel* it.

She heard a knight running for her, his plate clanging as he crossed the floor. She rolled, ignoring the pain in her arm as she made a massive swing, willing the wind from her blade. It leapt from the sword with a shriek, slamming into the knight's helm. He slammed onto his back, his helmet coming off as he scrambled to his feet. She was quicker, moving in to kill him, but the others were already responding, moving in with broad strokes of their swords to drive her back. Still, there was fear in their eyes. She smiled as they formed up again. It may not be all her powers, but it was *something* of the gods, the last sliver of luck she'd asked for.

She moved in again, no longer caring for their wind. She *leapt* into it, her sword transformed into a rudder on a river. It cut through their wind, absorbing it again as she passed through. And as she landed, she swung, slamming her wind into the knight in the center. This was her fight now, and she'd scared them, proven she could win as she marked all three. It showed in the way they moved, the knight on her right — the one bleeding from his knee — afraid to commit too much as he swung. She ducked under his blade, moving inside as she rammed her sword beneath his helm, dropping him in a gurgle of blood.

As the blade slid through, she was almost surprised. To trade so many blows, fight through so much wind, the lethal blow felt less…*inevitable* than it usually did. It felt more like what it was in reality — chance. But there was no time to savor her victory, there were two more, and she used the sword's momentum to rip through the knight's neck, pulling her elbow back so she wouldn't get trapped in his helm. She turned again, tracking the other knights in her mind. She begin to spin, preparing to take more wind. She had to stay fast, had to move before—

There was a sword sprouting from her chest. She looked down at it dully, the surprise from her own blow still fresh in her mind. But this… Blood began to blossom from the wound, staining her tunic a deep red. There was a knight there already, stabbing through her with all his might. It was *her* who'd overcommitted, the knight she'd taken offering himself up to save his friends. Her hand reached for the sword, the blade digging into her palm as she struggled to remove it, her lungs searing as they failed to breathe beyond the steel.

Somewhere in her mind, she registered Teros's scream. She looked up, meeting the knight's eyes. There was no pity there, though there was…*something*, a chance for Teros?

"Please," she said, blood already filling her mouth. "The boy. Please."

But her voice was so quiet. She could barely tell if she was hearing her own words.

He tore his sword back out as she fell to her knees, her body impossibly heavy, a pool of her own blood already waiting for her on the floor. Finally, after everything, she was about to die. But she didn't feel the peace she'd expected. Instead, she could only think of Teros, the weight of regret pressing into her heart. She fell facing the window, the pillars staring at her through the glass.

Suddenly, their whispers came back to her, pouring into her mind. She wanted to laugh. All this time without their magic, and they came back to her now? But maybe the gods would save her boy. Maybe the gods would succeed where she had seen nothing but failure. If only she could know for sure.

"Please," she said, and her eyes went black.

33

Teros never stopped screaming. Even as they dragged him up the stairs, he screamed for all he was worth. Not that he thought it would save him. He didn't care about that. At this point, he'd rather die, anything to get the image of Eyri dying out of his head. It felt like Mother all over again, her blood running out over the floor of Uncle Pesrin's house. The two were entwined, ensnaring him in their awful hell. No, he didn't scream to be saved. He screamed out of rage, out of shock that the only thing he had left in this world could be torn away from him.

Still, the knights didn't silence him this time, didn't try to hit him over the head. They seemed shocked themselves, climbing the stairs slowly behind the man with the knife, dripping their own blood against the stone. It was only when they reached the top of the stairs, when Teros scrambled free, clawing at the hooded man's face, that the knights intervened. One of them punched him in the stomach, making him double over as they dragged him by the hair to the center of the room.

If only Eyri had listened. *Run* was what he'd mouthed to her with the knife against his throat. But their eyes had met too briefly and now she was gone. He stopped fighting, staring at the ceiling of the room. This floor was narrower than the others, its ceiling glittering with gemstones. When they finally stopped, he went limp, his head rolling to the side as he took in a giant altar. It glowed in the torchlight, no doubt one of the sacred metals. But sacred to whom? Where were his gods now?

"Do you speak Deynen?" the hooded man asked, looking down at him.

He nodded.

"Good," the man said, switching languages. "Hold out your hand."

He did so, the man pulling back his hood. Teros winced as he slid the knife across his palm, but he didn't cry out. It was nothing compared to what they'd done to Eyri. When there was a pool of blood on his palm, the man pulled out a glass vial, filling it as he turned toward the altar.

"I have to prime the metal," he said to the knights who were taking off their plate and dressing their own wounds. "Watch the boy."

They nodded, though they seemed to pay Teros no mind as they unwound their bandages. Maybe he should try to run again, try to fight — try to do *anything* — but he didn't have the strength. As his arm flopped back down onto the stone, he thought how nice it would be to never move again. They would kill him, and it would finally be over. Mother, Eyri, Borash. Finally, they'd all be together again.

34

Eyri woke to the sound of water. She was lying facedown, but the cold she'd felt seeping into her body was gone. Still, the ground was…soft? She blinked her eyes open, finding herself on a fine white powder. Was this…sand? She almost didn't remember the word, having to dredge it from the poems of the Wise Father. But he had crossed ground like this, hadn't he? When he left the Giant Lands and crossed a mighty desert. Perhaps—

She gasped, remembering the zinc knight's sword. She lurched to a seat, feeling at her chest, but there was nothing there. She looked down at her robes but there was no blood, she—

The blood suddenly reappeared, her robes stained red, but just as quickly, it was gone again. It was like she'd dreamt it. Except… *Teros.* It had to be real. He was in danger. Why had she stopped fighting? Where was she?

She stood, her head swimming as she looked for her sword. But even as her vision cleared, she stopped short, staring at the view. It was water, more than she'd ever seen. Like a river with no end, or a second sky. It was impossibly blue. It was…*perfect,* like nothing she'd ever seen.

Suddenly, she noticed a woman to her side. It was as if she'd appeared out of thin air, though it didn't startle her. Somehow, it was as if she'd always been there. She was sitting with her knees folded beneath her, her back to the water. Eyri found herself drawn to her, her feet moving without being told until she was standing before her. Without meaning to, she dropped to the ground, kneeling in a mirror image of the woman.

This was no normal woman. In fact, she might not have been a woman at all. She was impossibly beautiful, perfect in a way no human could be. And she was also hardly there. She was made of light, like the shape of a woman standing in the sun, or something you could only see from the corner of your eye. As Eyri watched, the woman flickered, seeming to become two, then three before returning to her normal shape.

The woman met her eyes, her gaze soft somehow even with a face made of light.

Sitosarunal, the woman said, though the words were more in her mind than

160

in her ears.

Suddenly, her vision hazed over, another image appearing before her of the pillar in the square, only it was glowing. The light seemed to pulse as if it were seeking something. But how could light do such a thing? How could a light have longing? It was steadier than a flame, the light shining in the same way each time. Still, the meaning of the word seemed to appear in her mind a moment later without her needing to think.

The one seeking is the one who is sought.

She didn't know what it meant, yet it filled her with calm. This was a presence that cared for her, even as it filled her with sadness.

"You're hurt," the woman said, suddenly using words she could understand. It was as if the strange word had bonded them, creating an understanding only they could share. She frowned, looking Eyri up and down.

"I…"

She remembered the sword running through her again, but where was it now? The memory felt distant.

Serushalenomay, the woman said, this time in her mind again. There was an image of women in a line, each one younger than the last as she rested her arms on the woman before her. *Daughter.*

Suddenly, it felt like the woman's eyes were boring through her. She knew everything about her, everything she'd suffered. And there was…pain in her gaze. This woman understood, she—

"Teros," Eyri said suddenly. "You have to help me get back to him. I have to save him, have to—"

The woman nodded. She *did* understand. There was nothing more important than the boy. She was like a mirror, and when Eyri looked in it, all she could see what Teros. He was *everything.* He was her heart, and she had to save him.

"We are weak," the woman said, her image blurring again before snapping back into focus. "I am not *Biralunai,* free to heal as I see fit. And this place…"

She gestured at the sand surrounding them. The woman looked up, and Eyri followed her gaze, only just noticing the sky. The horizon was bright, the sun still visible above the water, yet she could see the night sky, the blue somehow fading when she looked directly at it. It was full of stars, too many to count, thousands, millions of them. She recognized the Mother's Home, though most were in constellations she didn't know. Some of them were even strange, shaped like honeycombs, six pinpricks of light around a seventh in the center. They were scattered throughout the sky, though there seemed to be no pattern to how far each one was from the next.

"I'm afraid it won't be much," the woman said, calling Eyri's attention back from the stars. "I was broken like the others, but perhaps, with my sister…"

The woman looked to her right, and suddenly, another woman appeared, though she was hazier than the one across from Eyri. The first woman met her eyes again.

"You're sure this is what you want? You could rest, you know. It isn't normal to speak to me like this, to be so deep within, lost to your own *welloshara.* And even more…"

The woman cocked her head, seeming to look *through* her.

"I've often wondered if I'd meet one such as you — not that I would question the truth of a vector, unlike the Unseen… Still, there is something in your mind, some story you tell yourself. Like the first story, the sword of light and shadow. *Teskorelonai.*"

An image appeared in her mind. It was a broken jar, cracks across its surface, yet she somehow knew it still held water.

"Perhaps you *could* wield a different blade, but much pain awaits if you return. I ask again, daughter, are you sure?"

"I'm sure," Eyri said.

She looked down, suddenly noticing her hands were full. In her left hand was a seed, and in her right was a mask. It was cold porcelain, the face of a Masked One. But the seed was warm. It was like a star someone had shrunk to the size of a button. She looked up, expecting the sky to have one less star. Instead, she found a swirling darkness. It was invisible save for the way it spun in the sky, swallowing strands of light from the stars closest to it.

Somehow, staring out at that sky, she knew she could plant the seed in her heart and enter that darkness. She could be gone from this place, gone from everything. It would take her pain away, take away everything she'd ever suffered. But…she *wanted* to suffer. If it meant having Teros back, she would take any amount of pain. She would even wear the mask again if she had to.

Gerotusanayil, the woman said, but it seemed like her voice was coming from the seed now. *A choosing,* it seemed to mean.

"Choose," the woman said again in Eyri's own tongue. "Choose, and know you've set your own path."

"I choose him," Eyri said, looking up. "I choose the boy."

The woman smiled.

"So be it."

Eyri gasped, her lungs burning as they filled with air, like the atmosphere suddenly had a mind of its own, forcing her chest to rise. She felt a searing pain in her heart just as an impossible cold filled her body. She doubled over on her side, her mouth moving inaudibly from the pain. She could still feel the wound in her chest, but it was closing, stitching together of its own accord. And just as quickly as it began, it was over.

She pushed herself to a seat, her vision blurry. She felt at her chest, and it was still sore, but the wound was really gone. She peeled back her tunic, the cloth slick with dark blood. There was a bright red line in the middle of her torso, and she could feel the weakness in her core, like some of the muscles hadn't reformed. Was this what the woman meant? She'd said it wouldn't be much, that pain would be waiting for her on the other side. She—

She looked up, seeing the pillar directly across from her through the giant window. Had that woman…? She blinked, her vision swimming as the old whispers poured into her mind. This time, though, it seemed she could understand what they were saying. Like the woman on the beach, each word filled her mind with images, blurring from one into the next until, suddenly, there was silence. But in its wake...*power.*

She could *see* the air around her, her body thrumming with Identity. Even without food, spending months without enough power to feel even a trickle of magic, it was there all the same. It was like the day in the temple, when her magic somehow held beyond her food, allowing her to save Teros. And she would save him again. The gods had answered. Even if it was like no god she'd ever heard of... Who was that woman? Certainly not one of the Elders. Maybe it was the Sacred Mother herself, but for the moment, it didn't matter. She had power, and Teros was in trouble.

She stood, her legs shaking, but the air held her up. She found her sword. She felt a...cringe from the pillar, its whispers hesitant. The sword meant death, the mask she'd held in her hand in front of all that water. Was it wrong to kill? Or did the woman simply mourn the loss of life? Still, she'd been given a choice, and she would choose Teros every time.

35

Eyri walked toward the stairs, suppressing the urge to run. The desperation was still there, her love for Teros, but she could feel how weak she was too. Despite the incredible power pouring through her mind, her body felt like an eggshell someone had already cracked. Still, she felt lighter somehow, too, the air seeming to move out of her way, the threads of Identity parting it like silk. It was ten steps before she realized she wasn't breathing. She'd been moving air in and out of her lungs with magic, her mind — or the gods? — forcing her to breathe.

She stopped, closing her eyes as she forced in a breath. She felt a searing pain, but she swallowed another lungful of air, pushing the pain down. Weak as she was, she *needed* to breathe. Some part of her knew this much power couldn't last forever, and she had to be ready to win this fight when the gods left her again. She shook her head, feeling sharper from the pain, her mind clearer. Even as the Identity had kept her alive, something about breathing with magic hadn't been enough.

She looked up the stairwell, her eyes flooded with strains of Identity. Still, she felt she *knew* the air now — knew what it wanted, what it was capable of. An image of the woman on the sand flashed back into her mind.

Serushalenomay, the woman said again. *Daughter.*

"Thank you," Eyri whispered, forcing in one last searing breath. It was time to fight.

She *leapt* up the stairs, cutting through the air like a kite, her mind parting the air before her and pushing with the air behind. The air seemed to tear like it had before, a thunderclap following in her wake as she cleared the stairwell. It was just as well, too, because it seemed she hadn't had another moment to spare. The two knights were bent over Teros, their swords in their hands. As she landed on the tile above, they looked up, their eyes wide. The third man had removed his hood, but he looked up from a silvery altar, backing away.

"Anndem," the knights said in unison, though their words hardly had time to register as she *seized* the air. Part of her could feel the world outside, the swirling sea of gas rising into the sky. Even as it seemed to go on forever —

strangely stopping just before the stars — it was a distant thing. For a single moment, all she needed was this one room, and with a goddess in her mind, she could touch every breath of air at once. Wrapping Teros in a bubble, she pulled the boy toward her just as she pushed outward with everything she had.

The tower shuddered, the air clapping with the power of a thousand storms. For a moment, there *was* no air, every line of Identity pushing to the other side of the room, flinging the men through the air like playthings. In the wake of that awful thunderclap, she almost lost herself, felt herself pulling into the void in the air. Something told her the world wasn't meant to be so empty, though she'd always taken for granted just how *full* the world was with gas. Still, the goddess seemed to hold her together, keeping her from disappearing into that void. As air filled the room again, rushing through the cracks in the masonry — and any other hole it could find in its desperation to refill the room — she felt her power fade.

Serushalenomay, the voice said again. Somewhere in that word she found a truth — she was herself again. She had chosen to live, and that meant she must be separate from the gods. Still, even though she couldn't force the air to move around her, she found her spirit bursting with Identity, like a wellspring of a thousand chul'uns she knew would never run dry. The goddess may still be looming in her mind, but she would have to win this fight herself.

She looked down, finding Teros at her feet. She released the bubble of air around him, and he scrambled to his feet.

"Eyri?" he asked, burying his face in her chest. She felt hot tears against her robes, though it was only a moment before he pulled back again, feeling where her wound had been. "But you... Is this real?"

She actually laughed, something she never thought she'd do again. Even as it pulled at her wound again, it felt good. It felt *real,* allowing her to stop being a god and just be...Eyri.

"The gods came for us," she said, dropping her sword as she pulled him close again, her hand rubbing the back of his head. Had his hair always been this soft? How had she lived without hugging him every day? How had she convinced herself there was anything more important than him? Still, she couldn't stay this way forever. Across the room, the knights were stirring, groaning as they got to their feet. The third man had disappeared, though there were alcoves all around the room, little doors behind the thrones she'd scattered. Oddly, the altar hadn't budged despite every other thing being flung about.

Part of her wanted to turn back down the stairs and run, to be done with all this fighting, but these men had seen their faces, knew what she could do. She couldn't leave without finishing this, and the knights seemed to know it too, picking up their swords as they dropped into their stances.

"Hide in the stairwell," she said to Teros, positioning her behind him. It was time.

The knights didn't bother with formations this time, throwing as much wind as they could at her, but even without touching the goddess directly, it was a laughable amount, a breeze compared to her storm. As their wind reached her, she batted it away, the power dissipating as if it had never been. She ran at them and slid, whipping herself forward with a powerful gust, her back become a sail as she tore across the room.

Rattled as these men were, though, her body felt incredibly weak. Perhaps it would be a fair fight after all. She came up in a swing, powering her sword forward with her wind more than her muscles. It hit the knight's blade with a clang, her wrists aching at the contact. It was enough power to throw the knight back a good foot, but his partner was already on her. It would be hard, but after so many months with no magic at all — and dozens dead below killed with nothing more than her sword — it felt *good* to fight this way again.

With wind to support her, she could lean back further to dodge the knight's swings. It was like having an extra leg, allowing her to twist and weave through the air. It let her swing harder too, letting her fight one at a time instead of two, the men unable to coordinate their attacks when they were struggling to keep their footing under her blows. She kept pulling at her well of Identity, but it never lessened, never hit her with the Passing either. It was almost as if she were nothing but a vessel, channeling the goddess like the caves around the sacred river. And as she felt for the magic in her mind, she found something else — *Remembrance.*

She thought of the other woman on the beach, the one who'd flickered out of view the moment she appeared. Was each Principle connected to one of those women? She'd thought the magics were from the elders, but what if they were from the pillars themselves? It—

She didn't have time to think of that, not with these knights to deal with. But she reached for the Remembrance on instinct. It wasn't bottomless like the Identity was, but there was *a lot* of it, five hundred chul'uns at least. She poured it into one of the knight's arms as he swung, freezing it in the air with nothing to stop her as her own blade flicked across his neck, dropping him to the ground.

She could sense the other moving up behind her, the wavering of the air warning her of his final, desperate attack. The same tactic was what had killed her down below just moments ago, but she was a different person now. She seized the air around her, *thickening* it somehow, the opposite of the airless void she'd created just before. It slowed his sword just enough to let her spin, ducking his blade as she came up with her own, taking him in the throat.

His eyes met hers as he bled out, his blood covering her gloves. She felt…sad, horribly sad at killing this man, though she wasn't sure if that was her or the Identity. Perhaps it was the memory of her death, the only time she'd ever truly lost a fight, had ever had to consider what came after. Still, wherever it came from, the pity was real. She eased the man to the floor, holding his hand as his eyes glazed over. Only then could she let go, slumping to the floor as her own lungs heaved, the wound in her chest searing with pain.

It was done. It was finally done.

36

"Eyri?" Teros asked, sticking his head above the banister. The sounds of fighting had stopped, and he didn't want to be away from her for another second. It was surprising he'd agreed to hide at all, surprising he would let her risk herself again after just losing her. But…she was *different* now. He didn't understand what she'd said about the gods, but he still understood power, and what he'd just witnessed was unlike anything he'd ever seen.

He saw her in the middle of the room, the knights dead at her side. At first, his heart leapt with fear, seeing her sitting on the ground, but she turned to him and smiled, motioning for him to join her. He ran across through the wreckage of the thrones, caring little for the shattered glass and tile between them. She opened her arms and he hugged her, squeezing her until she coughed and he finally let her go. Still, he felt *whole* again, the voices drifting back up from the bottom of his mind, content to no longer have to lie.

Together, they whispered. *Together.*

"We have to go," Eyri said, coughing again. "There'll be more knights, and I don't know if I can fight anymore."

"I can get you out," a voice said from behind the altar.

They spun, finding the hooded man from before, the one who'd taken the blood from his palm. Teros's hand was a bloody mess, but he lunged for Eyri's sword, getting in between her and that man. He would never let her fight alone again.

"Now wait, lad," the man said, putting his palms up. He glanced at Eyri before looking at Teros again, speaking quickly in Deynen. "I'm sorry about before, but those knights made me do all that. I'm a man of…of *science*, I suppose, but also a priest, and what I saw here today… I've been looking for a way back to the gods, and I guess you're it."

"If your priests take blood from children, we don't want any part of it!" Teros spat. He was suddenly filled with rage, so much he scared himself. Even if what the man said was true, he was still part of everything that had happened, everything that had almost taken Eyri from him. "Give me one reason I shouldn't run you through right now."

"It was all the knights," the man said, his throat bobbing as he gulped. "Really. But I promise I can help. Listen, there's guards outside already. I can get you to the tunnels, but without me, I'm not sure you'll get out of here alive."

"Guards?" Eyri asked in Zennan, her eyes wide as she apparently understood that word at least. She held her hands out, and Teros helped her to her feet. She put up a hand as the hooded man moved forward, freezing him where he stood. She walked over to the window, looking down below as she swore.

Teros joined her, his stomach dropping at what he saw below. There were hundreds of palace guards and nearly a dozen knights.

"I have supplies," the man said from behind them, "and places to hide. Please, I want to get out of this basin as I'm sure you do. Just give me a chance. I…think the gods have chosen you and not me. Just give this old man an ounce of mercy."

"What is he saying?" Eyri whispered.

"He says he can get us out."

She took a deep breath, closing her eyes.

"Okay," she said, turning to the man as she nodded. "But anything funny and I take you through the heart before I die."

Even in a foreign language, the so-called priest seemed to understand her threat, bowing low in the Zennan style. It was an odd sight from a Deynen, not least of all from a man who'd only just tried to kill them.

"I swear on my life," the man said. "Follow me."

He crossed the room at a jog, opening a door behind one of the fallen thrones. It led to another staircase, a narrow one descending into the dark of the inner tower.

"Come," Eyri said, taking her sword as she pushed Teros ahead of her. "Everything will be fine."

Teros hesitated, unsure he wanted to risk taking his eyes off her ever again. But when he looked back, she only smiled. His heart was pounding, but for the first time in months, he believed her. Somehow, everything *would* be alright. The gods had given Eyri back, and he had another chance, a way to get everything right. He would be a better friend, a better son. They could be a family again.

"Together," he whispered to himself, following the man into the darkness of the tower. "Together."

THE END OF BOOK II

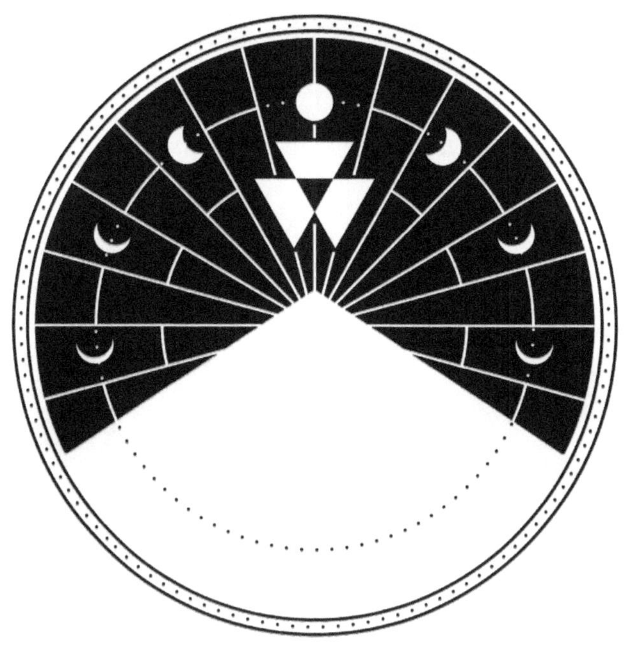